Lock Down Publications and Ca$h
Presents

I0666779

OPPS
CRY TOO
PART 2
STANDING ON BUSINESS

Written By
SAYNOMORE

Copyright © 2025 SAYNOMORE
OPPS CRY TOO 2

All rights reserved. No part of this book may be reproduced in any
form or by electronic or mechanical means, including information
storage and retrieval systems without permission in writing from the
publisher, except by a reviewer who may quote brief passages in
review.

First Edition 2025

Printed in the United States of America

This is a work of fiction. Names, characters, places, and incidents either
are products of the author's imagination or are used fictitiously. Any
similarity to actual events or locales or persons, living or dead, is
entirely coincidental.

Lock Down Publications
P.O. Box 944
Stockbridge, GA 30281
www.lockdownpublications.com

Like our page on Facebook: Lock Down Publications
www.facebook.com/lockdownpublications.ldp

Stay Connected with Us!

Text **LOCKDOWN** to 22828 to stay up-to-date with new releases, sneak peaks, contests and more…

Like our page on Facebook:
Lock Down Publications

Join Lock Down Publications/The New Era Reading Group

Visit our website:
www.lockdownpublications.com

Follow us on Instagram:
Lock Down Publications

Email Us: We want to hear from you!

PROLOGUE

Cash walked past the apartment window and heard a little girl say, "I'm hungry. Can you please get me something to eat?"

Cash stopped walking and looked at Symone and turned around and walked down the stairs to the apartment. He opened the door and heard a man say, in a loud voice, "I told you I'll get you some food when I'm ready! Now take your ass in the room!" He then heard a loud smack and someone hitting the floor and a door slamming.

Cash walked into the living room and looked at the dirty apartment. It was a mess in there— trash was everywhere. He walked to the kitchen and saw a man with a crack pipe in his hand and a lighter, and a female on the floor high out of this world.

The man looked at Cash. "Man, who the fuck are you?"

Cash pulled his gun out with a look of death in his eyes. "Symone, go check on the little girl."

The man dropped the crack pipe on the table as Symone walked into the room. The little girl was on a mattress on the floor with no sheets on it, wearing dirty clothes, crying with blood from her lip from when the man smacked her down. Symone grabbed her hand, picked her up and walked out the room with the girl on her hip to Cash.

Cash looked at her then he smacked the man in the face with the gun, knocking him down to the floor. "You got money to get high with but you don't have money to feed her. Then you hit her like she a fucking man."

The little girl was hiding her face in Symone's shoulder as Cash was yelling at the man, pointing his gun at him.

"No, it ain't nothing like that, man. I was going to feed her in a little while," he said with blood all over his face, in the corner of the kitchen floor.

"I hate motherfuckers like you with all my fucking heart. Then you put your fucking hands on her 'cause she was hungry, nigga."

"I didn't mean to do that; that was a mistake, man."

Cash pointed his gun at the man's face. Symone walked to the window and closed it. She looked at the radio and turned the music up loud and covered the girl's ears. Cash looked at her when she did that.

"Yeah, and so is this, motherfucker." Cash pulled the trigger, shooing him 2 times in the head, killing him. Blood splattered all over the back counter. He then looked at the little girl's mother who was so high she ain't know what was going on. "Take the girl to the truck and pull it up front now."

Symone walked out the apartment with the little girl on her hip. She put her in the truck and pulled it in front of the apartment.

Cash saw the truck was there. He grabbed the mother by her arm and dragged her to the truck and put her inside. He walked back down to the apartment and grabbed the mother's purse and walked out of there, closing and locking the door behind him. He got into the truck and Symone pulled off

She looked at Cash. "Where are we going?"

Cash looked at the little girl then back at Symone. "My house."

Symone ain't say another word. She just drove the truck. She never saw Cash act that way before. It was the first time she saw him spazz and it wasn't about money or drugs.

Chapter 1

Symone walked up to Cash as he was on the deck smoking a blunt at his house. "Cash?"

Without turning around Cash said, "Where is the little girl?"

"She in the bed sleep. I washed her up, washed her hair, fed her and laid her down. After she ate, she went right to sleep."

"And the mother?"

"She locked in the room downstairs, still high as hell. She don't know what's going on. She not even in her right state of mind."

"Have Kado and Soulja clean the body up. The keys are in her bag on the counter to her spot. Then I want the whole spot cleaned out. I want everything in the trash. I want you to pay all late fees for rent, water etcetera, etcetera."

"Okay, I'll get on that now." Symone wanted to ask him so bad why he was doing this, but she knew not to question him.

***

Big Apple looked at the money and kilos on the table as the workers were counting the money up and breaking down the kilos of cocaine. Cash was right. 100 kilos turned into 200, and over the last year, they took Brooklyn by storm, dropping bodies and taking over block. The Go-Gettas—

their name died out. Nobody flew their flag. And if Cash saw you with the colors on, you were getting rolled. Symone was cooking up 10 to 15 kilos every three days. Cash's little homie Kado's gunplay was dangerous. Soulja and Amen had the work in his hands, guaranteed to make the drop. Browns ran the streets and every-fucking-body knew it.

"Big Apple, you want me to make that drop to Soulja? And pick that bread up he got over there?"

"Nawl, Test. We will pick that baby love up Saturday. I only want to do one pick up a week. We going to keep shit running smooth the way it's been."

"Copy that."

"But make sure you have all your bags ready for your drop offs this weekend, homie."

"Already. I'ma get on that one."

Big Apple ain't say nothing he just nodded as Test walked off as he lowered his head and lit his blunt.

***

Gangster lowered his head, sniffed a line of coke then sat back in the chair. He was on America Most Wanted for killing a cop but he ain't give a fuck. He was going to hold court in the streets and be judged by bullets than to be judged by 12 and sentenced by one.

Tasha walked in the room, sat on his lap and kissed him on the lips. "Baby, you know I'm down for you but your name is Gangster. You can't keep hiding out like this. If you going to be on the run, at least let's get some money, but sniffing lines of coke and fucking all day and watching the news ain't doing it for me now more."

"Tasha, my face is all over the fucking news. I can't show my face right now. It's only been a year."

"So don't show your face. You was a boss. You had the streets on lockdown. You just need to play the boss role again."

"And how I'ma do that? I don't have nobody but you I can trust."

"My little cousin Savage and his right-hand man Jamaica. They 'bout that life and they always wanted to get down with you growing up. I can bring them over here so you can meet them. I know you will like them."

"Even so, I don't have no work to hold the block down at all. It's still a dead-end."

"Maybe not. My home girl Nicole said that one of Cash workers name Amen be pillow talking."

"Word? What that nigga be talking about?"

"So, last weekend she wanted to go out, but he said she can't. She asked why and he told her every Saturday Test drops him and Soulja off 15 kilos and picks up close to 600K."

"Why would he tell her all that?"

"Because she a bad bitch and she got that wap."

"You know what? Bring her and your peoples over. If shit is the way you say it is, we are about to get this paper."

"Alright, daddy. I'm about to call them now."

"Good, go do that." Gangster smacked Tasha on the ass as she got off his lap to make the call.

***

Cash sat at his table eating with the little girl watching cartoons when Symone walked Monica to the table. Monica looked at her daughter laughing and eating as she sat.

"Hey, mommy."

"Hey, baby." Monica looked at Cash and she knew he was pissed off.

"Symone, take Adrian into the other room to finish eating and watchin' cartoons."

"Okay. Come on, princess. We are going to go into the other room, okay?"

"Okay."

Once they walked out the kitchen, Cash pulled his gun out and placed it on the table, pointing it at Monica.

"Cash, please don't do this. Please, don't."

"Why the fuck shouldn't I take your life? You are doing it to your-fucking-self already."

"I'm sorry. After B-God was killed, it was so hard on me. Then Jason came along and told me he got us, and I started using and it got out of control. I don't know who I am no more."

"I don't give a fuck about your cries or tears. I walked past your spot and heard that little girl say she was hungry and Jason yelled at her. So you know what the fuck I did? I walked in your house and killed his pussy ass for putting his hand on my dead homie baby girl." Cash got up from the table, picked the gun up and walked right up to Monica. He put it to her lips.

Monica had tears in her eyes. "Open your fucking mouth, bitch."

Monica started crying as she opened her mouth.

"Suck on it. and I ain't going to tell you again." Monica was sucking on the neck of the gun when Cash said in her ear, "If you ever let a man put his hands on her again, I will fucking kill you. If I find out you are on drugs again, I will fucking kill you. You are going to stay here with me and your daughter for the next 90 days 'til I know you are clean. Do I make myself clear?"

Monica nodded.

"Good, because when this gun cum, it's going to be a bullet to the back of your fucking head." Cash pulled the gun out of her mouth. "Make you a plate of food then go enjoy a meal with your daughter in the other room."

Monica did what she was told as Symone walked up to Cash.

"If you want to know who she is, she B-God baby mother and that's his daughter. Even in the grave we take care of our own."

"I respect that."

"Good because I'ma need you to lace the apartment out for me and make sure you get both of them all new shit. When she cleans herself up she going to come work for me."

"So you can keep an eye on her?"

"Facts. Hands down." Cash put his hand on Symone's shoulder before walking off.

Chapter 2

Detective Cross walked to his wife's headstone with flowers in his hand and a bag in his other hand with a toy truck and doll for his son and daughter. He had them all laid to rest right next to each other. He laid the flowers down then the doll and truck. With tears in his eyes he said, "Baby, I'm so sorry I wasn't there for you when you needed me the most. I'm so-so sorry. Everyday it pains me to know that you and the kids are gone. Please, if you can hear me, find it in your heart to forgive me. Please let the children know that I love them."

Detective Cross took his two fingers and kissed them and placed them on the headstone of his wife and children. He then said the Lord's Prayer before getting up and walking away. It's been a year since his family was murdered and three more families after that. He knew this serial killer was going to see prison because he was going to kill him personally; the same way he killed his wife and kids. That was a promise he made to himself.

***

Gangster was smoking a blunt, looking out the window when Tasha walked into the apartment along with Savage, Jamaica and Nicole. Nicole was bad as hell. Brown skin, long honey brown hair, hazel eyes with a Coca-Cola body. Savage was light skinned with long locs and a tattoo under his eye of a black heart. Jamaica also had locs but he was slim built, dark skinned with a cold grill on his face. Tasha walked up to Gangster and kissed his lips as she introduced him to everyone.

He walked up to Savage and Jamaica and gave them a pound. "Yo, I appreciate y'all pulling up. Y'all know the lifestyle I live and how I give it the fuck up."

"Word, I already know how you give it up. I heard about how you bodied that CO. Left that motherfucker choking for air," Savage said as him and Jamaica dapped each other up.

"Yeah, I know about you too, Gangster. Your name goes hard in these streets," Nicole said.

"Respect, beautiful ladies and homies. If y'all trying to get down with me, I'm letting you know now I body shit for real and I need killers around me. No softhearted niggas and no sensitive ass females or niggas. If y'all 'bout that life, let's run up a bag and catch a few bodies on the way."

"Hell yeah. I'm ready to eat, homie. I don't give a fuck who have to take a dirt nap," Savage said.

"What about y'all two?"

"Shit, I'm with it."

"Me too. You rocking with my girl, you rocking with me."

"Good, because this ain't no walk in the park. Everyone gets their hands dirty and bloody to wear that green flag. Nicole, the ball's in your court. Tell us what we need to know to start eating. Tell me how deep his pillow talking go." Gangster pulled the blunt and looked at her as she started to talk.

***

"Yo, Amen, how we looking over there? Test be here tomorrow night for the pickup?" Soulja yelled out to him.

"Shit smooth over here. It's 450K with 2 birds left."

"Say less. We should have that off tomorrow by the time he makes the drop off." Soulja looked down the hall. It was crackheads lined up waiting to get high, side by side. Soulja had the spot airtight. He had work to sale to the crackheads and to supply the dope boys who wanted weight. No one seen his or Amen's face except the guys who he put on. He had 3 more spots where he sold the most out of, so 9 out of 10 times he was posted up here.

"Yo, Soulja, I'm about to go get something to eat. You good."

"Yeah, I'm straight. Hurry your ass back so you can break them kilos down."

"Already. I got you." Amen walked out of the trap through the back door. Once outside he pulled his phone out and called Nicole.

She picked up on the third ring. "Hey, daddy. What's up?"

"You tell me. You are blowing my line up and I'm at work. What's goodie?"

"I just wanted to hear your voice, that's all. You don't have to be rude and shit."

"It's nothing like that. I'm just getting ready for the drop off tomorrow and I need to make sure everything is good. Look, meet me at the pizza joint on 10th Avenue. I'm on my way there now."

"Okay, I'll be there in 10 minutes."

"Cool." Nicole hung up the phone and looked at Gangster. "Nicole, do you know where they do the drop offs at?"

"No. There's a cut he be taking to on the low, and I think it's where he do the drop off at."

"No pressure. Jamaica, when he leaves the pizza spot, follow him. He might lead you to where our pot of gold is going to be at."

"Say less, but we need to be moving now though. He said ten minutes."

"Yeah. Y'all go take care of the business." Gangster watched as they left, knowing shit is about to be on and poppin' real soon.

Chapter 3

Gangster stepped out of the SUV with his hood on. Along with Tasha, he walked into the projects. He had eyes all over him from Animal crew. He walked up to his door and knocked two times. One of Animal's guards opened the door and looked at him, then Tasha.

"You going to let me in, Killer?"

Killer looked back at Animal. "It's Gangster and a chick."

"America's Most Wanted Gangster? Let the celebrity in."

Killer moved out the way for Gangster to walk past him.

Animal smiled and clapped his hands as Gangster walked into the spot. "Loyalty is a motherfucker. There is a $300,000 bounty on your head. You lucky I ain't one of them rat motherfuckers looking for a little pocket change." Animal walked up to Gangster and gave him a pound.

"That's love, family. How you?"

"You know, getting money, staying low-key. I see you staying low-key, too, if they ain't get your ass yet, but for you to show your face knowing you are hotter than the sun, there must be a reason."

"Yeah, there is. I need a favor."

"And what's that?"

"I need some hardware. Some heavy shit. M16, AR15, MAC-11 with rounds."

"You talking over $15,000 in hardware. What you getting ready for a war?"

"Just some unfinished business I need to take care of."

14

"Look, I'm going to give you two of everything, plus 3000 rounds and, I'm going to throw in two black nine millimeters, $30,000 back. And since you are on the run, I'ma give you 90 days to pay me back."

"I can do that."

"I know you can, and one more thing, Gangster."

"Yeah, what's that?"

"Don't show your face around here no more. You hot and I don't need the police watching my shit. Send baby girl back with my money. I know her face now."

"Say less. I respect that."

"Yo, Killer, get this man what he needs." Animal looked at Gangster and winked at him as he walked off.

***

"Look. Make the drop off to Amen first. They low as hell right now. Soulja called and told me he was on the last two yesterday. Then make the other drop offs," Big Apple said as he passed the duffle bags to Test.

"Already. I'm about to do that now. I'll call you after I make my first drop."

"Say less then." Big Apple dapped Test up before he walked off.

Test placed the duffle bag that was going to Soulja in the front seat and the other two in the backseat. He pulled his gun out and placed it on his lap and drove off. Amen was out back waiting for Test. He lowered his head and lit his blunt. Soulja was watching everything in the surveillance camera as he passed the workers the last bit of cocaine that was bagged up. You had Savage and Jamaica on the left side in the cut with the murder one mask on, then you had Gangster on the right side with the green flag covering his face. Test pulled the black jeep up to the back of the trap. He stepped out holding the duffle bag in his hand.

15

Amen stepped off the back steps holding the duffle bag with the money inside. Savage looked at Gangster. Gangster nodded. That's when Savage came out blasting. He wasn't doing no talking. By the time Amen saw what was going on, he was shot in the chest and arm. Test pulled his gun out and was shooting back. Gangster came from the side and hit him up with the MAC-11. Test dropped his gun and yelled as his body hit the ground. Jamaica ran and picked up both bags. Soulja opened the back door, shooting a Glock-40 at them with two more guards. Bullets were flying everywhere. Gangster and them shot it out with them until they were in the clear. All you heard was the car's tires peeling off. Soulja ran to the middle of the street, shooting at the car until it was gone.

"Fuck! Fuck!" He ran back to the back and saw that Amen and Test were still breathing. He opened the back door to the Jeep and saw that there were two more bags. He threw them to one of the guards as they got Amen and Test inside the Jeep. He backed it up and took off, headed to the hospital. He pulled his phone out and called Cash.

After a few seconds, Cash picked up the phone. "Soulja, talk to me."

"Yo, we was just fucking hit. Motherfuckers got us for the work and cash."

"What the fuck you mean you was hit?"

"Niggas came out of nowhere, clapping. Test and Amen got hit up. I'm on the way to the hospital now with them."

"Fuck. Okay. I'm on my way to the spot now."

Soulja hung up the phone and looked at Test and Amen. "Hold on y'all. We are on our way to the hospital now. Just hold on," he said as he was running red lights trying to get them there.

Chapter 4

Cash looked at the videotape of the whole thing 3 times. This was a planned hit. His guys ain't know this was coming. They were ready. They knew about the drop and pick up. Even worse, the time. He turned around and looked at Soulja. "What's the condition on Test and Amen?"

"Both of them are in ICU right now but Test is in a coma. He got hit up bad."

"You know who did this?"

"Hell no. If I did, they would be ducking bullets right now."

"I know who did this shit."

Soulja looked at him crazy. "Who then, so we can lay they ass down?"

Cash acted like he ain't hear what Soulja said. "How much money was in the bag?"

"580K."

"580 and 20 kilos. But you know what's crazy? They ain't even know about the kilos in the Jeep. They only knew about what was to be dropped off here. I want more guards around the clock here. I got to make a phone call; I'll be back." Cash walked out the spot and called Big Apple.

After a few rings he picked up. "What you find out, Cash?"

"It was Gangster. He was the only one wearing a green flag. It's like he wanted me to know it was him."

"So, this pussy ass nigga is back. Check the move. You want me to put Kado on the block?"

"Yeah. Let's see what the streets is talking about."

"I'm putting that call in now."

"Good. Hit me when you know something, because someone is about to open up shop somewhere soon."

"And you know we are going to be right there at the door."

"Fucking right. Call me when you find something out."

"Copy that."

Cash hung up the phone and pulled his cigar, knowing NYC streets were going to become body land again.

***

"Now that's what the fuck I'm talking about. We don't do no talking, we pull up, pop out and lay the fucking murder game down. Now that's how the fuck we eat," Gangster said as he puffed on his blunt, looking at Savage and Jamaica pulling the money and kilos of cocaine out the bag.

"Shit was wild. I saw how you ran up on son and hit him with the Mac-11. That shit was a Kodak moment—something out the movies," Savage said.

"That nigga screamed, his body hit the ground, and I know it was over," Jamaica said as he laughed.

"Check this shit out real talk. If y'all niggas are going to get down with me, I need loyalty. I need to know I can trust y'all. If I got a enemy, y'all have a enemy. That's how that shit rock."

"Man, we down for you, bro. You say get 'em, we going to say got them. We here, on God."

"That's why I fuck with you, Savage. I respect your heart."

"We ten toes down with you, bro. Facts."

"That's all the fuck I needed to hear." Gangster walked up to both of them and handed them green flags with a smile on his face. "Y'all niggas is Go-Gettas now, for life. It ain't no turning back, and the only way out is with a fucking bullet."

"Shoot or get shot."

"Fucking right, Savage."

"So, let's get to this bag now."

"You know what, Jamaica? Now you are fucking talking. Y'all niggas take a bird a piece for yourself for putting that work in, and 30G's apiece. Also, I need you to count out 90 stacks of 30. We have to pay Nicole and Tasha, and Animal for the guns and the rest of the baby love. I'ma get us a trap spot and some workers to run shit. We about to take NY over."

Chapter 5

Tasha walked in the projects looking like a supermodel with her outfit hugging her hourglass body. Tasha knew she was a bad bitch. She walked up to Animal's door and knocked two times.

Killer opened the door and looked at her. "Animal, it's baby girl. Gangster little buddy."

"If she's here she must have a present for me. Let her little sexy ass in."

Tasha walked past Killer into the room on the left where Animal was at. She'd been around niggas who got money but Animal was cut different. She had never seen so much work and money in one spot before.

"You have something for me?"

"Yeah, I do." Tasha reached in her bag and pulled out the 30G's and passed it to Animal.

"Damn, he got this back within 48 hours. What the fuck he do, rob a bank?"

"I don't know what he do. I don't ask him no question because it ain't none of my business."

Animal waked up to her and said in her ear, "I like that. A badass bitch that know how to mind her business."

"That's how you suppose to stand on business. You see it, you don't see it. You hear it, you don't hear it."

"I like that. If you ever trying to get some money on the side, pull up on me and I got you, super star."

"So, you have a number?"

"Just knock on the door. I'll be here."

"I got you then."

Animal watched as Tasha left knowing a bad bitch like that ain't nothing but trouble but Tasha was so bad he wanted to see what she was built like.

***

Kado walked around Brooklyn trying to see what the streets were talking about but they were dry. Nobody was saying a word. Big Apple already poured him a drink and told him it was Gangster, so he really was looking for motherfuckers flying green flags. He posted up at the deli when he saw Nicole pull up. She stepped out of a gray Lexis looking like a Barbie doll from head to toe. She was fly and iced out. He saw her before but he didn't remember where. He pulled out a cigarette and walked off as he lit it. He pulled out his phone and called Big Apple.

After a few rings he picked up. "Apple, I been through and nobody is talking at all."

"Niggas is quiet right now. Give it some time. Niggas are going to talk."

"Say less. I'm about to head back to the other spot now."

"Do that. Just keep your ears to the ground."

"Copy that." Kado hung up the phone and walked back to the trap spot trying to remember where he knew shorty from.

***

"Symone, I been watching this video for a while now. How the fuck do Gangster come out the blue with hardware like that, and who are these little niggas behind him? What the fuck I ain't seeing?"

"You know what, Cash? I don't know why I ain't think of this before. Gangster is cool with Animal, and Animal be having all that shit."

21

"You fucking right. Animal. I can see him giving him that shit now."

"And I know where his main spot is."

"No, don't worry about that right now. We are going to take care of Animal. What we need to find out is where is he moving my shit at and who are these little niggas he have running with him."

"I can put my ear to the ground and see what I can found out."

"Do that and go by the hospital and see if Amen is able to talk."

"Alright." Symone walked out the room leaving Cash in his thoughts.

Chapter 6

"You want $36,000 for a bird? You breaking the bank, Rip. That's too fucking much and you got Savage letting them go for $30,000 right now."

"Who the fuck is Savage? And where this nigga at?"

"Over there off of 110th Street. Look, Rip, I'll do $34,000. If you can't do that, then I can't fuck with it."

"Yeah, I'll do $34,000 for you. And you said this nigga name is Savage and he's on 110th Street?"

"Yeah, a little young ass nigga. He over there poppin' his shit. Light skin nigga with long locs, green flag tied around his hair."

Rip had a smile on his face when he said that.

"Fuck that nigga. Come on so we can take care of the business." Ant ain't know he just opened up Pandora's box, running his mouth off.

***

Symone walked into the hospital up to the 3rd floor where Amen was. She walked into the room and looked at him laying in the hospital bed. She walked up to him and rubbed his hand.

Amen opened his eyes and looked at her. In a low tone he said, "Symone?"

"How are you holding up in here?"

"It hurts to breathe. This shit hurts, Symone."

"I know it do, but you strong. You got to hold it down. Remember you are a soulja. A fucking goon."

"Sometimes it's fucking hard. The doctor said I will never walk the same again and he don't even know if Test is going to wake up. He have a thirty percent chance of living."

"He's good. He's going to make it. He's tough. Listen to me. I need to know how they knew about the spot. Did you tell anybody?"

"No, I ain't tell nobody about the spot. I don't know how them niggas found out. They just pulled up clapping."

"They must have been following Test. That's the only way they could have known about the spot."

"That's the only way, Symone."

"Yeah. Look, close your eyes, get some rest and I'll be back in a couple of days to check on you."

"Okay."

Symone kissed Amen's forehead and went to talk out the room. When she saw his screen saver it was a picture of Nicole. She thought nothing of it when she walked out the room.

***

"Detective Cross, you been working day and night for months straight. You need to take a break on this case."

"Captain, respectfully, my wife my kids are dead. He sent a video of them calling my name, saying, 'Help me, daddy,' as he cut open their throats. He was targeting me alone and I know this is some bullshit that Detective Boatman got me pulled into from being shot 12 times to my family being killed. So, please don't tell me to take a break. Let me have my peace as I work on this case."

Captain Moore knew he was right; she could never imagine the pain, the feeling he was going through to see his kids crying for his help and there was nothing that he could do to save them. Without saying a word, she just walked out the office knowing he was right.

***

"Yo, yo that genie came out that bottle. So word on the streets is there's a little nigga named Savage moving work on 110th Avenue flying green flags. Kado and Symone, go check that shit out. Rip, I need you over there with Soulja. Kado, if shit is what they say it is, body season. Big Apple, you know I been dealing with some personal shit. As soon as I get shit right, I'll be right here, back by your side."

"I already know, playboy. Go take care of your business and when you get shit right, pull up on us. We got this shit."

Cash dapped Big Apple up and walked off.

Chapter 7

"Mommy, is this our new house?"

Monica looked around Cash's house then back at Adrian. "No, baby, it's not. We just staying here for a little while."

"I like it here. I don't never want to leave."

"Baby, mommy have to go to the bathroom. I'll be right back, okay?"

"Okay, mommy."

Monica walked to the bathroom and closed the door. She placed her hands on the sink and looked at herself in the mirror and cried, thinking about what drugs had done to her life. Just to support her habit she stole, sold her body, and sucked on so many men she lost count.

Cash walked past the bathroom and heard her crying. He knocked two times then opened the door and looked at her. "You good, Monica?"

Monica shook her head. "Cash, I'm so sorry you had to see me like that. It's been nights that I thought about killing myself because I let the drugs take full control of my mind, and to think about what my baby girl been through because of me. I'm just so sorry."

"Monica, we all have our ups and downs. You been here with me for a little over 30 days and look at you. You already getting yourself back together. I just need you to do right by Adrian. That's what I need you to do more than anything."

Wiping the tears out her eyes Monica looked at Cash. "I am. I promise I'm done with drugs. I swear I am."

"I believe you, but I still want you here with me a little while longer."

Monica nodded. Cash kissed her on the forehead and walked off.

***

Gangster had his eyes closed as Tasha was sucking on his manhood. He had his hand on her head as he was stuffing her mouth with his thick manhood. Tasha's eyes were bloodshot red with tears coming down her face as he was choking her with his dick. He pulled out of her mouth and started kissing her as he pulled her up to her feet and bent her over the bed. She arched her back for him as he played with the tip of his manhood against her clit before sliding inside of her.

"Damn, baby, this fat dick feel so fucking good inside of me. I can feel you in my stomach, baby."

"Who pussy is this?"

"It's yours, baby. It's your pussy."

Gangster placed his foot on the bed. He wrapped his arm around her waist and started pounding her harder and harder.

Tasha was letting out loud moans. "Baby, I'm about to cum all over this dick!"

"Cum on daddy's dick then, sexy." Gangster held Tasha close as he came deep inside of her. He pulled his dick out and saw all the cum on it. He smiled and smacked her ass. "Damn, baby, you got that fucking wap."

"Daddy, you got that dick that make this pussy cream."

"Let me go take a shower then I have to go check on Savage to see how that money is flowing over there."

"Do you want me to come with you?"

"Hell nawl. We will never get up out that motherfucker if you do." Gangster got up and walked to the shower.

Tasha laid back down thinking about Animal and how much money she can make with him.

***

"I can say they got the block pumping. They are getting to the bag over here."

"Yeah, they getting some money, but I ain't see this nigga Savage yet, Kado."

"He's going to be coming around real soon."

Symone lowered her head as she went to roll up a blunt. That's when Kado tapped her leg.

"Look at that Lexus that just pulled up. I seen it before."

Symone looked at the Lexus. "Yeah, we found the niggas that hit us. They couldn't wait to spend that money."

"And this is the second time me seeing shorty get into that car. I just don't know where I seen her at before."

"Yo, I know I'm fucking tripping now. That's the bitch that Amen got on his phone as a screen saver. I just seen it yesterday when I went to the hospital to check on him."

"So now we know how they got the drop on us, Symone. Amen was pillow talking to his little bitch." Kado pulled his phone out and took some pictures of the car and Nicole.

"So you ready to ride down on them?"

"Nawl. Chill. They got too many guns. Let's see what Cash and Big Apple say first."

"Shit, then, let's get the fuck out of here." Kado looked one more time before driving off, headed back to Big Apple.

Chapter 8

Cash sat in the chair with his hand on his head listening to Kado and Symone. He looked at Big Apple and nodded. "Symone, are you sure this is the same bitch that's on Amen phone?"

"Hell yeah, I'm sure. She the same female in that picture on Kado phone."

"Big Apple, what you think?"

"Ain't shit to think about. That Lexus is our money. That ice this bitch is wearing is our money. That dope them crackheads is smoking is our bricks, and this nigga Amen was pillow talking, so we lost out on $2.5 million because of this nigga. I'm about to go to the hospital and kill this pussy nigga."

"Say less. You go handle that business and I'm going to see about this bitch nigga Animal to see what part he play in this shit. Rip, I want you and Kado to send a message to this nigga in the gray Lexus. Symone, you and Soulja stay at the spot. We still need to let the block know we run this shit." Cash looked at everyone and walked off, knowing shit was about to go boom.

***

"How the fuck we looking over here?" Gangster said as he walked in the door.

"Nigga, we need a re-up. That's how we looking. Shit, we down to our last five bricks," Jamaica said.

"That's what the fuck I'm talking about. How much money we got over there, Savage?"

"350K right now, but like Jamaica said we still have five more bricks to go."

"Cool. Let me go make a call. I'll be back in a few minutes."

"Shit, you know where we are at," Savage said.

They had the block beating. Everyone was pulling up. They had cash, dope, and lower prices. They were winning all the way around the board.

***

Big Apple walked into the hospital up to the 3rd floor. He looked at Amen sleeping. He picked up his phone and saw the same picture of Nicole. The phone was locked. He placed it back down and woke up Amen.

Amen opened his eyes and looked at him. In a low tone he said, "Big Apple?"

"Yeah, it's me, little homie. How you holding up in here?"

"I'm good for the most part. Y'all found out who hit us up?"

"Yeah, we did. It was Gangster with the help of you."

"What you mean? I don't fuck with Gangster. I would never turn on you and Cash."

"Remember I used to tell you family business is family business?"

"Yeah."

"You was talking about family business outside of the family to baby girl you got right here on your phone and she set you up, Amen."

"Hell no."

"Yeah. Hell yes. She riding around with the same motherfucker who shot you and Test up."

"Big Apple, hear me out—"

Big Apple cut him off. "Amen, you was pillow talking and the bitch you loved fucked you over. Rule number 1 in this game: Trust no bitch. Now you put me in a fucked up position."

"I can make this right. As soon as I get out of here I'm make it right."

Big Apple walked to the side of his bed. "You can't make this right, but I can."

"Big Apple, I can. I swear to God I can."

"No, you can't." Big Apple grabbed the pillow and covered his face with it and held it there until he stopped breathing. Once he stopped breathing, Big Apple picked up his phone and pressed his thumb against it and unlocked it and walked out the room like he was never there.

***

Cash stepped out of the G-wagon and walked into the projects smoking his cigar. He walked up to Animal's door and knocked two times.

Killer opened the door and looked at Cash. "Damn, Cash. Long time no see. Come in."

"Yeah, it's been a minute, Killer. Animal available?"

"Yeah, let me get him for you." Killer walked off to get Animal for Cash.

"Don Cash, what do I owe the pleasure?"

"You can say I'm just window shopping. You never know what I might need in a few days."

"Well, you know I got whatever you might need, and if I don't have it here I can get it for you in a few days."

"Animal, how long we knew each other for now?"

"Over 15 years."

"And I always came with my paper up front to your door."

"You have, but what you getting at?"

"Last week one of my spots was hit. 580K and 15 kilos were taken and two of my men put down. You wouldn't know nothing about that would you?"

"You know, now that you said that, Gangster pulled up on me last week and got some hardware from me on his face. Then, two days later he came and paid me $30,000. I'm not saying he hit your spot, but it might be something to look into."

Cash knew Animal was telling the truth. "Yeah, I think I'ma check into that. Good looking, family."

"You know how I move. If I get a location on him, I'll give you a call."

"That's love."

"Yeah, but love comes with a price. You like some of this hardware over there?"

"Yeah, I do. Matter of fact..." Cash pulled out $20,000 and handed it to Animal. "I don't ride dirty. I'll send someone back to pick up what I purchased."

"Love is love. I'll make sure they get it to you."

Cash dapped Animal up and walked out his spot.

Killer walked up to Animal. "So what you thinking, boss?"

"Gangster name is about to be put to the test once again because when Cash sends his shooters, they don't miss. Get Cash order ready for him."

***

"Savage, how much you said was over there? 350K right?"

"Yeah, on the head, and we still got more bread coming in."

"Cool. Jamaica, come with me so we can pick up the rest of the cake. I'll do a count then we will call the plug and get this work."

"Fucking right." Jamaica got up from the chair and passed Savage the blunt. He dapped him up as he walked out the building with Gangster.

Gangster threw his hoodie on as he walked out the doors.

"Kado, that's Gangster right there with the green and black hoodie on carrying the bag over his shoulder."

"So, the nigga that's with him?"

"A bullet-catcher because he's going to catch all these bullets to his fucking chest."

"Symone, you crazy as hell. You ready?"

"Yeah, let's make a snake out of these niggas."

Kado opened the car door. Both of them had brown flags covering their face. They ducked as they were alongside a few cars. Kado came from the side of the car and yelled out, "Browns, motherfucker!"

Then, all you heard was the sounds of guns blasting. Symone ran from the other side of the car shooting Jamaica 3 times in the shoulder, back and leg as he was trying to run. Gangster dropped the bag and pulled his gun out and was shooting as he was running backwards. Symone ran and picked up the bag. Kado started shooting out all the windows to the building. Gangster jumped behind an electric box as bullets were flying his way. Symone stood over Jamaica as blood was coming out of his mouth and pointed the gun at his head. Savage came out the door shooting an M16. Jamaica looked at Savage. Symone shot him in the jaw. Kado and Savage were having a shootout. Symone started shooting at Savage. He ran back inside. Kado and Symone took off running to the car. They got inside and Kado peeled off. Savage opened the door and ran up to Jamaica as he was shaking out of control. Then you heard the sounds of the police coming.

Gangster ran up to Savage. "Yo, listen. He's gone. I got to get the fuck out of here and you got to go get that work before they kick in the door, now!"

"I swear I'm going to kill these niggas for you, bro. I got you. I love you."

Gangster took off running, so did Savage, 2 minutes right before the police pulled up, jumping out of their cars.

Chapter 9

Tasha knocked two times on Animal's door before Killer opened the door for her.

He smiled as he let her inside. "You know where he is at. He's in the back room. If I was you, I'll knock before I walk in."

Tasha nodded and licked her lips as she walked past Killer. She walked to the door and knocked twice. She then opened it. She knew what she was doing. She was being nosey. Animal came from the bathroom with just a towel on around his waist. His body was dripping wet. Tasha couldn't help to lust over his chocolate body. She was looking at his jet-black curly hair, his dark brown eyes, to his full goatee down to his amazing chest covered with tattoos and his full six pack. She was lost in her thoughts looking at his broad shoulders and arms. Her thoughts were interrupted by his deep voice.

"I see you came back. Close the door. I ain't dressed."

Tasha closed the door. "You said if I wanted to make some money, so I want to see what you had on the table."

"I need a driver. Whatever they spend, you get ten percent. Bare minimum you might make in one day is $5,000. The most is $20,000. How that sounds to you?"

Before Tasha could say anything, Animal took his towel off and started drying is hair with it, showing off his thick, long manhood. Tasha thought that Gangster had a big dick, but Animal was just as big as Gangster when it was soft, and

Animal wasn't hard. Now she knew why they called him Animal— because he can touch places with his dick that Gangster could never.

"If I do, this is between me and you, not me, you and Gangster. Just me and you."

"That's the only way I do business. When I call you pick up, and from now on, your first name is on point and your last name on time."

"I got you. So, when do I start?"

Animal walked to the nightstand and picked up a knot of cash and handed it to Tasha. "That's $10,000 right there. Where your phone?" Tasha handed Animal her phone. He placed a number inside. "I put my number in there as Uber, so when you see that number make sure you pick up. And if you can't pick up, you have 10 minutes to call me back."

"Okay, I got you."

"Tasha, if you fuck me, I will have pleasure in killing you. That I promise you."

"There's only one thing we all have in this world and that's our word, and I stand on mines ten toes down."

"Good. I'll be in touch."

Tasha looked at Animal's dick one more time before walking out of the room. She wanted to fuck him so bad but she had to keep herself together. She was new to the crew and she had to earn her respect and it wasn't by getting fucked in.

***

Big Apple watched as Kado and Symone walked into the warehouse. Symone had a bag over her shoulder. Big Apple looked at Cash and winked.

"So how that shit go?"

"Like a box office hit. We ain't do no talking. Symone laid one of them niggas down and grabbed the bag. Gangster, as the fuck nigga, took off running."

"What's in the bag?"

"I don't know, Big Apple. I never looked in it. I just know if he was carrying it, it was something worth having."

Symone took the duffle bag and threw it on the floor next to Cash's feet.

Cash bent down and opened it and smiled as he threw a stack of money to Big Apple

"It looks like y'all caught him when he was trying to re-up. That means he's low and just eyeballing this money. It looks like 250K; somewhere in that neighborhood."

"So, what now?" Kado asked.

"I'm waiting on a call from Animal and a pickup I sent Soulja and Rip to take care of."

"And what about Amen?"

Cash looked at Big Apple.

"He like to pillow talk so I let him talk to the pillow. You don't never have to worry about talking to that nigga again." Big Apple threw Symone Amen's phone. "Take care of that bitch on the front."

"Say less. I got it." Symone and Kado went to walk out when Cash called Kado.

"You said Symone killed that dude?"

"Shit, that nigga was on the ground fighting for his life."

"That's understandable, but if he ain't dead, make sure you finish the job. You can find him at the hospital in ICU."

Kado ain't say nothing else. He just turned around and walked off.

***

Gangster paced the floor with his gun in his hand, smoking a blunt when Tasha walked into the apartment. He looked at her and snapped. "Where the fuck you been? I been blowing your phone up all night!"

"My phone was dead. What the fuck is wrong with you?"

"While you was out doing what you was doing with your dead fucking phone, bullets was flying at me and Savage, and they clapped the little homie Jamaica up and got 350K from us!"

"Who clapped at y'all? Who was it?"

"Cash sent his shooters." Gangster pulled the blunt.

"So where is Savage at now?"

"He's at the other spot right now laying low."

"I'm about to go over there now."

"Wait, wait, wait. Hear what I'm about to say. I need you to go to the other spot and get the $430,000 out the safe and bring it to me. I have to meet the plug in like 3 hours and we need this re-up. The streets is hot. I can't show my face right now."

"Okay. I'll go do that now."

"Thanks, baby. I swear you be coming through like the starting five off the bench."

"You know I got you, daddy." Tasha walked out the apartment knowing Gangster needed her right now more than ever, and she was about to ride for her nigga. Do or die.

Chapter 10

"Death comes in many styles. Me, myself, I like to use this knife I been using it for the last year and a half. It's just the feeling I get when I feel someone's warm blood running down my hands. Now that's a feeling that's better than pussy." He ran the knife along the side of her cheek bone and gently down her chin until the tip of the knife was on her neck.

She had tears in her eyes as she sat in the chair, tied down. She closed her eyes and took her last breath as the knife jammed into her throat and cut it open.

He looked at the other 3 dead bodies as he laughed and walked around the house. He wrote on the wall, "Detective Cross, I'm back," in her blood. "Felt just like your wife's blood running down my hands." He then put a smiley face with tears coming down its face as he walked out the house in the night's air.

***

"Soulja, how we looking over here?" Cash asked him as he looked around the spot.

"Shit smooth again. Rip got the spot on lock and we got cameras where we can see up and down the block now."

"That's what I'm talking about. How much money we pulling in a day?"

"Close to 70K," Soulja said as he pulled his Newport.

"That's cool. We got some of that money back. Kado and Symone put they murder game down and got 350K back and popped on them niggas that got Test."

"Damn, nigga, you should have let me handle that. That one was personal. Real talk."

"Nawl. I need you where you are at now— getting this money for the family. It's 'cause of you we are moving the way we are now. I need you to keep this baby love flowing."

"Respect. Cool. Any word from Test?"

"Yeah, he good. He tough. He's going to make it."

"That's what I wanted to hear."

"Look, I'm out. You know how to reach me if you need me."

"Copy that, family." Cash dapped Soulja up as he got ready to walk out the spot.

***

Detective Cross just looked at the writing on the wall. He was standing there for 20 minutes in silence, just looking until Captain Moore walked up behind him.

"We been here over three hours. You been standing here for the last 20 minutes. The bodies are gone. CSI did all they can do. It's time to leave."

"He's been quiet for the last 7 months, now he just pop up out of nowhere, and he's calling me out. He's haunting me."

"We are going to get him. I promise you that."

"No, Captain. I'm going to get him. I promise you that." Detective Cross walked out the house and looked at all the people standing around. He walked to his car and got inside to open up the glove box and took his bottle of brandy out and took a shot, then put his car and drive and drove off.

***

"Tasha, you mean to tell me Cash knows it was Gangster who robbed him?"

"Yes, girl, and Jamaica got shot up and they got 350K back. I just dropped Gangster off the last 430K to re-up with so we can still eat." Nicole looked out the window as Tasha was driving through the hood.

"So, what Gangster going to do about Cash? Because they probably know it was me who set everything up and I know you heard that Amen was killed in the hospital last week."

"Look, I got us. Trust me. I'm already working on some new shit. We good. You have my word."

"What about Soulja?"

"He straight. I talked to him already, too."

"Fuck it. I know you got my back, girl."

"Facts." Tasha pulled up to Nicole's spot and let her out the SUV.

Symone just watched as she walked into her house and Tasha pulled off. Symone said to herself, "Baby girl, your time is coming real fucking soon." She looked through Amen's phone some more to see what other address he had in there that they ain't know about, thinking of a way to set Nicole up and Cash wanted it to be bloody.

Chapter 11

Mac-Ru waited at the auto part shop for Gangster to show up as he smoked his cigarette. That's when he saw the shop's garage doors opening and the SUV pulling in. He saw Gangster and Savage stepping out of the SUV and Gangster holding a duffle bag in is hand as he walked up to him.

"America's Most Wanted. Gangster, what's good, baby?"

"Just trying to live and stay the fuck out of the police eyesight."

"I know what you mean. Who's your homie here?"

"Savage. He's my lieutenant on my frontline."

"One thing I can say about you, you always stayed with them killers. So, talk to me. What you trying to cop?"

"I need 40 bricks."

Mac-Ru rubbed his hands together. "40. That's a good number. You got the bread for that?"

"I wouldn't be here if I didn't." Gangster passed him the duffle bag.

Mac-Ru opened it up and looked inside then he smiled at Gangster. "Gangster, I like the way you do business." Mac-Ru passed the bag to one of his goons. "Yo, do the count and bring him his product." Gangster watched as his goon walked off. "So, you taking shit back over?"

"I'm just planting my flags again. Letting niggas know we still here."

"I respect that shit. Real talk. You been hearing about that serial killer? The motherfucker just killed a family of four a few days ago."

"Real talk, I heard about that shit. Some motherfuckers are just sick in the head."

Savage never said nothing. He just watched everyone's movement. That's when Mac-Ru's goon came back with the kilos in the bag. He passed the bag to Savage.

"You know what, Mac-Ru? I like the way you do business, too."

"You already know how we get down. Stay low, and if you see them boys in blue, shoot first because you are wanted dead or alive. They just want a body."

"You already know it's going to be a fucking war in the street before they take me to jail."

"Already. Stay up, homie." Mac-Ru dapped Gangster up before he walked off.

Once in the SUV Savage looked at him. "We are about to take shit by storm, but we got to hit them Brown niggas back. They got the homie in the hospital on his last leg."

"War cost money. Let's run this bag up first then we start knocking these niggas' heads off."

"Let's get it then."

Gangster turned the music on and pulled off bopping his head.

***

Cash looked down at Adrian as she sat on the floor quietly. "What's wrong, beautiful? Why you look so sad?"

She looked up at Cash. "I don't want to go back there. I want to stay here with you."

"I think you are going to like it. Trust me."

Adrian nodded.

"Come on, now. Let's get you into the truck." Cash picked her up and carried her to the truck. He looked at Monica and got into the Range Rover before pulling off.

Monica had been clean for 90-plus days. She didn't even look the same no more. It took them 30 minutes to pull up at the apartment. All eyes were on the Range Rover when it pulled up. Cash stepped out and looked at everyone with an ice-cold grill. He opened the door for Monica. When she stepped out, all eyes were on her. She was bad, looking like Megan Good in the flesh. Cash picked up Adrian and carried her downstairs to the apartment.

When he opened the doors and stepped inside, Monica couldn't believe what she was seeing. The apartment was laced out from a 62-inch flat screen on the wall in the living room to the black leather couch set and matching end table. Cash spent over $20,000 on the apartment.

Adrian ran into her room. He decked her room out in Disney's Princess and the Frog. She came out the room yelling to Monica. "Mommy, mommy! Come look at my room! Hurry up!"

Monica walked into the room. She had tears in her eyes looking at what Cash did for them. Cash walked into the room behind them. Monica turned around and looked at Cash.

"Monica, come let me talk to you for a second."

"Adrian, mommy be right back." Monica walked out the room and looked at Cash.

"You see what I done here, right?"

"Yes, and thank you so much. I really appreciate it."

"Monica, remember our first conversation at the kitchen table. If I have to, I will raise Adrian by myself. I don't want no drug dealers by you or her. Both of y'all have clothes and food. The rent is paid up for the year. I'll see you soon."

"Okay, and I promise you I'ma do right by her. Now can I pay you back?"

"I know you will, and in a few days, I'm going to come get you because you are going to come work for me. One day I might need you."

"Okay."

Cash kissed Monica on the forehead before walking out of her spot. Cash looked at all the niggas standing around and he said, "If I catch any of y'all down there or even trying her, my face will be the last face you see before you go talk to God."

Nobody said nothing as he got in his Range Rover and drove off.

Chapter 12

Tasha looked at her phone as it was going off to see the name Uber. She looked at Gangster as him and Savage were cooking up the work.

"Gangster, I'm going to the store. I'll be back in a few."

"Cool. I'll see you when you get back." Gangster walked up to Tasha and gave her a kiss before she walked out the door.

Tasha walked to her car and called Animal back.

After a few rings he picked up the phone. "You ready for your first run?"

"I'm on my way to you now."

"No, don't come to me. Go to 1051 Brook Avenue. In the parking lot there's a black van. The keys are taped to the front right fender above the tire. Take the van to Newark, New Jersey. Call me when you get there."

"Cool." Tasha hung up the phone and did what Animal told her to do.

The van was nice. She got the keys from where he told her and she drove off. It took her a little bit over an hour to get there. Once she hit Newark she pulled her phone out and called Animal.

After a few seconds he picked up. "Damn, you move fast."

"No. I'm just on point and on time."

"Oh yeah, I see you being funny. I like that. You are going to 21 Hillside. There's an Ace Center there. Pull up around

46

back. When the back doors open, pull up in there and just wait, okay?"

"Cool. Am I asking for anybody?"

"No. Just do as I told you. That's all."

"Okay." Tasha hung up the phone and pulled into the Ace Center. She waited for the doors to open and she pulled inside. There were four dudes in there.

One of them walked to her door and looked at her. "You can step out the van. It's going to be a while."

"Okay." Tasha stepped out of the van and watched them open up secret departments. They were pulling guns and kilos of cocaine out. When they were done, Tasha counted up 60 kilos of cocaine and 27 guns. She couldn't believe all that was in the van.

The same guy walked up to her with a smile on his face. He handed her an envelope. "There's $20,000 in there for you and Animal. Money is in this black duffle bag. Make sure he gets it."

"I will, and thank you." Tasha got back in the van and pulled off. Once she made it to her car, she locked the van up and put the keys back where she got them from. She placed Animal's duffle bag in the trunk of her car and pulled off. She called Animal and told him she will be there in 20 minutes.

Killer heard two knocks at the door and opened it and saw Tasha standing there. He moved out the way so she could walk inside. "I see the pretty face girl is back."

"Yeah, I'm back with your heavy ass black bag." She passed the bag to Animal.

He looked at her then opened the bag up. Inside were stacks of hundreds. Animal pulled out a stack of $100-bills and went to pass it to her.

She said, "I was paid already from the guys at the Ace Center."

"I respect your honesty, but when you do runs you get paid from both ends, so you good. Take this."

Tasha took the money and placed it in her bag. "Thanks. FYI, from now on can you give me a heads up? Like a few hours in advance, please?"

"Yeah, I got you."

Tasha smiled and walked out the door.

Killer walked up to Animal. "If she got paid, why you pay her again?"

"From the first time she was here, I watched the cameras. The whole time she was driving the van and after she made the drop, not one time did she go in my bag or ask no questions. She loyal and I need her to be around for a very long time. Come on, let's get this money counted."

***

Kado walked into the hospital and looked around at all the people standing around. Nurses, police officers, and patients. He walked up the stairs to the 2nd floor. He knew Jamaica was there. A bitch from around the way he used to fuck with worked there; he paid her for the information. She gave him his room number and all. Kado walked into the room. He looked at Jamaica asleep. He walked to the window and looked out of it to see if he saw his car. He then put on his gloves and open the window. He pulled his knife out his pocket, walked up to Jamaica and put his hand over his mouth. Afterward, he jammed the knife into his throat and pulled it to the side.

Jamaica opened his eyes as tears was coming down them and blood was pouring out of his neck. Kado moved his hand from his mouth and wiped the blood off the knife using Jamaica's bed cover. He then went to the window and climbed out of it to the ground. He looked around and started walking to his car when all he heard was a scream. He got into his car and drove off. There was no way he was going to make it out the front doors of the hospital without getting caught. She told him that since Amen was killed there, the nurse had to go into the room after every visitor, no matter how long they were there for, so the window was his only way out.

***

"Damn, I made $50,000 in just two weeks fucking with Animal. Damn, this money getting my pussy wet," Tasha said to herself as she opened up the safe in her room at her spot. She still had 20K and there and a kilo of cocaine she got Gangster for when they first did the lick on Cash's spot he never knew about. She looked to see that her phone was going off and that it was Gangster calling her. "Hey."

"What the fuck you mean hey. You left five hours ago talking about you was just going to the store. Where the fuck is the store at? Philly?"

"No, I went to the store, dropped the food off at my house, laid down and fell asleep. Shit, I was tired. I ain't know I had to check in with you every time the wind blows a different direction."

"You know what I got going on and you know we need you over here. You fucking tripping."

"I'm on my way back now, damn."

"Well get the fuck off the phone and get here then." Gangster hung the phone and lit his blunt.

He heard Savage yelling, "What the fuck? Fuck! Damn, homie! No, no, no!"

Gangster walked in the room to see what was going on. That's when he saw the news on the TV talking about how Jamaica was killed in the hospital today. Savage had his gun, walking back and forth in the living room with tears in his eyes, knowing his day one was just rolled.

"You get ready. When Tasha come here, we are going to go roll one of them nigga tonight."

"Fucking right, man. Somebody have to die tonight behind this one. On gang."

"Don't worry. We got this shit. On gang." Gangster handed him the blunt and walked off knowing his pain. The only difference is that Gangster rolled his right hand man for going against the family, but even then he still had tears in his eyes.

Chapter 13

"Soulja, this shit is crazy as fuck. Bodies is dropping like flies. The police is all over the streets again. Shit is wicked out here right now."

"Shit is most definitely crazy as fuck right now. You don't know when a nigga is going to pull up clapping."

Soulja just looked at the video cameras as he talked to Rip. "Yo, Rip, am I tripping or is that two niggas with the murder one mask on they face in that car right there?"

Rip looked in the camera. "Real talk, strap up. Them fools is about to try something." Rip grabbed his gun so did Soulja.

They rushed out the door, gun in hand with a few of their soulja's behind them.

Gangsta floored the car as Savage hung out the window, shooting two Mac-11s at them. As Soulja and Rip were shooting in the air as they were driving by, two of the guards were shot down. Rip ran to the middle of the street shooting the windows out the car. All you saw were the taillights turning the corner.

Rip ran back to the trap and shook his head at the two dead bodies. "Yo, grabbed they bodies and bring them inside before the police come here."

"Bring them where?" One of the guards asked.

"In the fucking building. Where else? Soulja, called Big Apple now and let him know what just went down." Rip ran inside the building and started putting all the kilos in duffle bags, knowing they couldn't use this spot no more.

***

Nicole heard a knock at her door. She looked out the window to see Savage's Lexus outside. She opened the door for him. Savage walked into her spot smoking a blunt. She could tell something was wrong with him. "Savage, what's wrong? Why you moving like that?"

"We just popped on Cash crew again tonight and I know I bodied two of them niggas." Savage sat down.

After saying that, Nicole looked at him lost for words. "Why? What happened?"

"You ain't seen the news? Them pussy niggas went to the hospital and poured Jamaica out. They killed the homie. You know I wasn't going to let that shit ride."

"Damn. Where Tasha and Gangster at?"

"Gangster at the new spot laying low right now. And, real talk, Tasha slick been MIA from time to time. I don't know what the fuck she got going on." Savage re-lit his blunt and passed it to Nicole.

"Well, you know you can always post up here to lay low if you need to."

"That's why I fuck with you so hard, Nicole. Real talk, you always got my fucking back."

"Come on. We Go-Gettas. You know I'm always going to have your back."

"Hands down." Savage got up and walked up on Nicole and grabbed her as he started kissing her.

Nicole grabbed him by the hand and led him into the bedroom. She closed the door and started undressing him. She loved the ink all over his body. She laid him down on the bed and started kissing all over his chest. She then stood up and got undress in front of him, showing off her hourglass shape. She dropped down to her knees and started sucking on Savage's manhood. It wasn't the biggest she had but he was thick and 7 inches long. Savage had his hand on her head as she was deep-throating him, taking her tongue around his dick, licking his balls and all.

"Damn, baby. I'm about to cum."

Nicole ain't stop. She just sucked on him harder and harder, jacking him off until he came all in her mouth. He had his eyes closed. Nicole tapped his leg. He opened his eyes and saw the cum all over her tongue. She swallowed it and smiled as she got on top of him.

***

"This nigga Gangster is starting to become a pain in my ass again. Fuck. From here on out, that spot is shut down. Symone, what you know about that bitch Nicole?"

"Cash, I know where the bitch lives and all. I'm just watching her, hoping she leads me to where the nigga with the Lexus stay. I know she got dropped off yesterday night by a black SUV, but I'm on that bitch body."

Cash nodded. "Good. Stay on the hoe. Soulja, start setting up shop at the other location. Rip, you and Kado hit the streets. I want to know where this nigga Gangster lay his head. Put a brick on his head."

Big Apple just smoked his blunt listening to what Cash was saying before speaking. "We need to promote violence. Stop all his money. Let the streets know if anybody shop or spend money with Gangster or his crew they are enemies of ours, and all our enemies catch bullets with they chest, and we ain't doing no talking."

"Y'all heard what Big Apple said. Put the word out on the streets." Cash walked up to Big Apple. "You know this is going to get messy right?"

"At this point, Cash, who give a fuck? We going to drop the bodies and let the police clean them up."

"Fuck it. Let it be a bloody summer."

"That's the best kind."

Chapter 14

Tasha watched as they counted up the kilos of cocaine and guns. This was the 6th run she made for Animal but she had a bad feeling about this one so she had her gun in her hoodie as she sat in the chair quietly and paid attention to what the two dudes were doing when one of them walked up to her.

"We are short 6 kilos and 3 guns."

"I have nothing to do with that. Everything that was supposed to be in there, I brought in to you. He told me it was there. That's something you and him need to discuss. I just need the money so I can go."

"You ain't getting no money until we get what we paid for, so you need to get the rest of our shit and come on back."

Tasha stood up. "Then you need to put the rest of that back where y'all got it from and I'll go talk to him and y'all can have the conversation y'all need."

"You don't get it. You are leaving and that is staying. Now get the fuck in the van!"

Tasha looked at both men standing in front of her. She turned around and put her hand on her gun. One of the guys grabbed her shoulder. She turned around real fast and shot him two times in the chest, killing him. The other guy rushed her and tackled her down to the floor. She shot him 3 times in the stomach. He rolled off of her.

She stood up and pointed the gun at his head. "No. You don't get it. Don't nobody take shit from me." Tasha shot him in the head, killing him. She run to the back of the van and started throwing all the guns and drugs in there. She looked around and found a blue tarp and threw it over the guns and drugs. She looked and saw a black duffle bag on the floor next to the table and saw it was full with cash. She put it in and ran and opened up the garage doors and ran back to the van and pulled off. Once in the van on the road, she called Animal.

After a few seconds he picked up. "Yo."

"Yo, these motherfuckers just tried to rob me, saying you was short 6 kilos and 3 guns."

"What the fuck you mean tried to rob you?"

"They said you were short and wouldn't give the work back. Then they told me to leave. One of them grabbed my shoulder so I pulled my gun out and killed him. Then the other motherfucker jumped on me, so I killed him, too."

"Fuck. I'm glad you got out of there, but where is everything at?"

"In the van. I just threw everything in the van and put a blue tarp over it. I grabbed the money and left. I'm on my way back now."

"Okay, okay. Look, don't come here. Go to the last location where we loaded up at before."

"You mean in Queens?"

"Yeah."

"Okay, good because I'm close by there now."

"Okay, I'll meet you there in 20 minutes."

Tasha hung up the phone and paced herself as she drove to the spot. That was the first time she killed someone. She couldn't believe all the blood she had on her.

Animal looked at Killer. "We have to go. Them damn Park Ave boys just tried to rob Tasha."

"What the fuck they got going on?"

"I don't know but she got the drugs, guns, and money and she on her way to Queens now."

***

"Yes, I'm looking for the Detective working the serial killer investigation."

The officer looked at the man standing in front of him. "Yes, hold on. Let me get him for you."

A few seconds later Detective Cross walked up to the older white male. "Hey, how can I help you? I'm Detective Cross. I'm working the serial killer investigation."

"Hey, my name is John Howard and I live on Ock Street. I work out of state often for IBM and I just got home yesterday. I was gone for two weeks. Long story, short I was checking my surveillance footage around my house and I think I may have something that can help your case if you care to have a look."

"Yes, yes. Please, come on back to my office." Detective Cross walked Mr. Howard to his office and put the disk in the laptop. He watched a single man who was about 6' 1" walking into the house. He came out 20 minutes later, then the house was in flames. "Damn, we know it's a man now, but we can't see his face. We don't know if he is black or white."

"Wait. There more, Detective."

They continued to watch the video and noticed the same man come back on the scene to watch what was going on. The only thing they knew now was that he was black or Puerto Rican because the camera caught his hand when he pulled it out the hoodie and walked off.

"Mr. Howard, did you show this to anyone else?"

"No, sir. I got it and brought it straight to you."

"Good. I don't need you showing nobody else this. I thank you for coming forward today with this information."

"No problem, Detective. I'm glad I could help."

"Here. Take my card if you need to reach me again."

"Will do."

Detective Cross walked Mr. Howard out and went to Captain Moore's office to show her the video tape of the serial killer.

***

Animal walked up to Tasha along with Killer and looked at all the blood she had on her. He took her gun and gave it to Killer as he hugged her. "Are you alright?"

"Yeah, I'm fine. I just never killed nobody before."

"Don't, worry I got you now. Wait right here," Animal walked to the back of the van and saw all the guns and drugs under the blue tarp. He then looked at Killer. "Yo, put everything where it needs to be in the other van and have the guys come and chop this van up. We can't use it no more. Then meet me back at the spot. I'm getting her out of here."

"Cool. I got everything under control here boss." Animal looked at Tasha, grabbed the duffle bag of money, wrapped his arms around her and took her to his car.

For 20 minutes straight they drove in silence to his house right outside of Queens. When they pulled up, Tasha looked at him. "Who house is this?"

"It's my house. Come on. Let's get inside."

When Tasha saw how Animal was living she couldn't believe it. His house was laced out. Animal took her by the hand and led her to his bedroom. Tasha just looked at him as he went into the bathroom. He came out a few minutes later and walked her in the bathroom and undressed her, placing her in the big jacuzzi.

"I'll be back in a few minutes, okay."

"Okay."

Animal picked up her clothes and placed them in the washer downstairs. Tasha heard him over the phone talking to someone. "No, what you don't understand is that your peoples tried to rob my Uber driver. You know how the fuck

I get down. If I was there, I would have killed them my-fucking-self, then any-fucking-body that looked like them."

"Animal, we been doing business for a very long time now. There was just a little misunderstanding, that's all. I'm sure we can work this out."

"There's nothing to work out. You knew the rules from the very beginning. Whoever breaks the trust or disloyalty takes the loss. And from this point on our business is done." Animal hung up the phone and threw it on the bed, and walked into the bathroom where Tasha was. "Do you mind if I join you?"

"No. Come on."

Animal got undressed and joined her in the tub. Tasha placed her back against his chest as he took the wash cloth and started washing her body. This is something Gangster never did.

"Tasha, I want you to know I'm really proud of you. You stood tall today, beautiful."

"I was scared."

"You don't never have to be scared again. I'm never going to let nothing happened to you, ever."

Tasha turned around and started kissing Animal deeply. She felt his manhood growing. She grabbed it with both hands. He picked her up and carried her out the tub to the bedroom. He placed her on the bed. Tasha let out a loud scream as Animal placed himself inside of her and started moving his hips in a circular motion. Tasha's mouth was open as her jaw was jittering.

"You deep-deep. I can feel you in my stomach."

"Get used to it. This is my pussy now. You always going to feel this dick." Animal started kissing Tasha as he started fucking her harder and harder.

She was moaning loud and scratching his back. Every time he was too deep inside of her, she started cuming all over his dick. Animal bit her neck as he was cuming inside of her. He pulled himself out and Tasha started squirting all over the bed. Animal started laughing.

"That's not funny. You have too much dick to be doing all of that, Animal."

"Come here, beautiful. Just come lay in my arms."

"No, come put your back against my chest, daddy."

Animal laid his back against Tasha's chest and closed his eyes. She put oil on her hands and was massaging his dick and balls nice and slowly as she kissed his neck. She had never been fucked like that before or held, and she ain't want the moment to end.

Chapter 15

Gangster picked up the phone and called Savage. After a few rings he picked up. "What's the word? How we moving over there?"

Savage pulled his Newport. "We ain't moving shit right now. Nobody is fucking with our campaign. Word on the block is there's a kilo on your head, and if anybody cops from us, it's shoot on sight. Them dope boys or crackheads ain't fucking with it."

Gangster closed his eyes and stood up and kicked over the living room table. "So the hood is saying fuck us?"

"Like I told you, shit is ugly as fuck right now. We might have to go out of town to move this work, fam."

"No, fuck that. Brooklyn is going to show us some love. Just be on point. I'll call you back in a few."

"Copy that. I'm here when you ready to make the next move."

Gangster hung up the phone and called Tasha. After a few rings she picked up as she was laying in the bed next to Animal who was sleep. "Hey, what's up?"

"Where you at?"

"My spot."

"Good. I need you to come to the spot. There's something I need you to take care of for me."

"Okay. Let me get up and dress and I'll be on my way."

"Cool. I'm waiting on you."

"Okay." Tasha hung up the phone. Her stomach was hurting and so was her pussy. She swung her legs out the bed and went to get up when Animal grabbed her arm.

"Where you going?"

"Gangster need me to take care of something for him."

"I need you to take care of something for me, too."

"What you need me to do, daddy?"

Animal pulled the cover back, showing that his dick was hard.

"Baby, my pussy is so sore right now, and my stomach is hurting from all that dick."

"So put your mouth around it. I need a nut before you leave."

Tasha ain't say nothing; she just lowered her head and started sucking Animal's dick. He grabbed her head and started fucking her face. Tasha was spiting all over his dick as he was choking her with it. He held her head still as he cum in her mouth. The load was so big it was coming out the sides. Tasha swallowed what she could as he pulled his dick out of her mouth.

Tasha took a deep breath. "Baby, your dick is too big to be doing all of that."

"Like I said, you have to get use to this dick. It's yours."

Tasha slowly got out of the bed and got dress. She loved Animal's vibe and how gangster he was, but he just had too much dick for her.

"Tasha, I forgot to tell you."

"What?"

"That duffle bag of money."

"Yeah?"

"That's your money, now. It should be 600K. I got my guns and cocaine back so I ain't take a loss. You caught two bodies and got my shit back to me safe. That's your money. You earned it."

Tasha couldn't believe what she was hearing. She couldn't stop smiling. "Thank you."

"No pressure. Just be on the look out when I call you."

"I will, daddy." By the time Tasha made it downstairs and out the door her Uber driver was just pulling up on her.

***

Nicole walked out her front door and got into a cab. Symone started the car and followed them. Cash let it be known that Nicole was a penny and that Gangster was the golden boy. He was the real prize. The cab stopped at Bulletproof Studios after 20 minutes. Nicole stepped out and went inside.

"Okay, baby girl, keep showing me the spots y'all be at. All I need you to do is lead me to the leprechaun wearing the green, baby girl." Symone still couldn't believe she was once Gangster's rider. She would have died for the set and all along he never gave a fuck about her. She was just a pawn on his chess board. In the back of her mind she really wanted to be the one to pull the trigger and kill his pussy ass for dogging her out all them years, then throwing her to the dogs as if she was a fucking bone. That hurt more than anything.

***

"You have to be fucking kidding me. So, all this time this sick son of a bitch comes back to the crime scene to watch and hear the cries of the victims' family from the sick shit he done did?" Captain Moore couldn't believe what she was seeing on the hard drive.

"So, we know he's 6'1", slim, but we can't tell if he is black or Puerto Rican. Captain, we can't put this on the news. That will let him know we are on to him."

"Yeah, I was thinking about that myself. What I'm about to say is really going to be fucked up but the only way to catch him is wait for him to strike again. And when he comes to see his work, we got him."

"I was thinking the same thing, Captain. I just don't want another family to go through that pain of losing a loved one in that horrible way."

"Just let me know what you want to do. We can air this on the news or we can play the waiting game. Just tell me what you want to do."

"Okay, just give me some time to think about it, Captain."

"The ball's in your court. You know where to find me."

"Yeah, I do." Detective Cross got up and left the Captain's office with a hard choice to make.

Tasha walked into the trap and looked at Gangster smoking a blunt, watching the news. She walked up to him and sat next to him on the couch.

"You good, beautiful? Why you walking like that?"

"My period came on last night. My stomach is cramping."

"Did you take something for it?"

"Yeah, I did. But what's up? What you need me to do for you?"

"I need a new spot to trap out of. I'm thinking shit is to hot out here right now. I need you and Nicole to go get a spot for me and Savage. We got too much work and we just sitting on it right now."

"When you want me to do this?"

"Like yesterday."

"Okay. Let me call Nicole and see where she is."

"That's why I love you, baby." Gangster placed the blunt down and kissed Tasha as if it was the last time he was going to see her. "Damn, baby, you really do love me."

"You know I do, sexy."

"Now go take care of that business for me and call me when you done."

"Okay, I got you." Tasha got up and walked back out the spot. She really did love Gangster but she knew there was no future with him. He was going to do life in prison or be killed in the streets. Either way, she knew they didn't have a future together. Once in the car she pulled out her phone and called Nicole.

Nicole picked up after the first few rings. "Hey, what's up, girl?"

"You busy? I need you to take a ride with me."

"Shit, no. I'm just cooling it. Come get me, girl."

"Where you at?"

"Your old stomping grounds. Bulletproof Studios and it's lit-lit in here right now."

"Shit, I ain't been in there in over a year. I have my reasons why, plus my dreams of being a rapper is over. That's been a dead dream."

"I hear you. How long before you get here?"

"Give me 20 minutes. I'll call you when I'm out front."

"Okay, I'm here."

Tasha hung up thinking how once in life that was her dream to be a rapper, but the night she helped Gangster kill Ray-J, that dream was nothing more than a dream to her.

***

Symone sat in the car waiting for Nicole to come out the studio. She rolled up a blunt and lit it. Her phone went off and she saw it was Kado calling her. She picked up the phone. "What's the business, Kado?"

"Just checking on you, making sure you good; that's all. I heard you was following that bitch Nicole around."

"Yeah, I'm watching this Barbie bitch, about to smoke this blunt and wait for her to come out of Bulletproof Records."

"Cool, just let me know if you need me and I'll pull up."

"Cool. I got you, homie."

"Peace."

"Peace." Symone hung up the phone and lit her blunt. That's when she saw the same SUV pull up from the other night. She put her blunt down in the ashtray and watched the truck. After a few seconds Tasha opened the SUV door and stepped out. "Wait. Fuck no. I know this bitch that Ray-J was fucking. Oh shit. Fuck no," Symone said to herself as she picked up her phone and called Cash.

He picked up after a few seconds. "Symone, what you got for me?"

"Remember the night Ray-J was killed? He said he was picking up his shorty from Bulletproof Studios?"

"Yeah, I remember that shit. Why?"

"The bitch that been picking Nicole up in the black SUV is this nigga girl."

"Hell nawl. You sure?"

"On Brown, I'm looking at this bitch right now."

"You strapped?"

"Always."

"Roll that bitch. It ain't hat hard to put 2 and 2 together to know that bitch set Ray-J up."

"I'm about to let this bitch body play catch with these bullets I'm about to shoot at her."

"Handle your fucking business."

"You ain't got to tell me but once."

Symone pulled her gun out and cocked it back and stepped out of the car.

Tasha looked at Nicole. "This nigga Gangster wants us to go to the Bronx and get a spot out there. I got an idea where he wants me to go, I just don't feel like taken that ride by myself."

"Girl, you know I got you. Let's ride out."

Symone came from around the corner of the SUV and pointed her gun. "Yo, bitch. Ray-J said what's popping!"

Tasha was stuck. Nicole jumped in front of Tasha as Symone was letting the shots off. She shot Nicole five times. Tasha took off running. Symone was shooting at her, hitting car windows as Tasha was ducking down. Symone saw people running out the studio. She started shooting at them, hitting one person, dropping them. She ran back to her car and drove off out the parking lot. Tasha walked back to the SUV and looked down at Nicole laying there dead with blood coming out her mouth with her eyes open. Tasha had tears in her eyes looking at her dead homie who died for her.

Chapter 16

"Big Apple, shit is crazy hot out there right now. The streets is flooded with police."

Big Apple looked at Kado as he was smoking his blunt. "What the fuck you mean? What happened out there?"

"I don't fucking know. All I know is that I hit Symone up early and she told me she was at Bulletproof Records watching the Nicole bitch, so I pulled up there because she ain't been picking up her phone and 5-0 is up there right now. They got the place blocked off. It was two white sheets and mad people standing around."

"And shorty still ain't picking up her phone?"

"Fuck no. I called her 20 minutes ago."

"Call her back and see if she picks up real quick."

Kado pulled his phone out and called Symone. After a few seconds she picked up. "Yo, Symone, where the fuck you at? I been blowing your phone up. It look like a war zone up there at Bulletproof Records."

'I'm on my way to the spot now. Shit got ugly. I ain't have time to pick up my phone before."

"Say less. Me and Apple is over here waiting on you now."

"Copy that. I'll see y'all in a minute."

Kado hung up the phone and looked at Big Apple. "She on her way here now."

"Cool, cool. We will find out the story when she gets here."

"Facts," Kado said as he pulled out a Newport and lit it.

***

"Savage, we going to get those niggas back for this one. My word to you."

Savage wasn't hearing nothing Gangster was saying. He was thinking about Nicole. "All we been doing is fucking talking. Jamaica dead. Nicole dead. We can't get this fucking work off. Cash is blocking us every time we make a move, and all you want to do is talk on broken promises. Newsflash, big homie, we up but we losing. Yeah we got work with the cost of bodies on our end."

"I been doing this shit for years. I know what it is like to take a loss. It's part of the fucking game. Shoot or get shot, and Jamaica and Nicole got shot. That's the up and downs of this shit. We can pull up on Cash and his crew like Billy the Kid and we are going to be laying right there next to Nicole and Jamaica on a piece of metal. Let me just get my thoughts together and I'ma tell you how we are going to do this."

"While you get your thoughts together, I'm going to go ride around. I need some fresh air. My fucking mind ain't right, right now."

"Savage, you can't have no feelings in this life. Remember that."

"Nigga, what the fuck you mean? I love that bitch," Savage said as he walked out the door.

Gangster looked at Tasha.

"He's right, Gangster. All you been doing is talking/"

"What the fuck you mean by that?"

"Nothing. I need some fresh air, too." Tasha walked out the door, leaving Gangster standing there.

***

"Savage, hold up. Let me talk to you."

Savage stop walking to let Tasha catch up to him. "What's up?"

"I don't need you out here doing nothing crazy."

"I'm 100. Real talk. I can't flex like this shit don't hurt because it do."

"Trust me, I know how you feel. I do."

"On some real hood shit, Gangster ain't Gangster no more. All this fool do is watch the news. He don't never leave the spot. I'm the one out here in the streets banging for the set, and we keep taken fucking loses back to back."

"Look, we are going to get those niggas."

"I keep hearing that shit but when? Jamica dead. Nicole dead. And those niggas are still getting money, moving work, smoking blunts, getting pussy—"

"Let me make a call and see what I can set up."

"Do that, but until then, I'm about to hit the block to see if I can move some of that work."

"Okay. Be on point while you out there."

"You telling me to be on point. Niggas just shot a cannon at your head. You need to be on point."

"I got this."

"Cool. Call me when you know something." Savage walked off to his car.

Tasha pulled out her phone and called Animal.

After a few rings he picked up. "I been calling you all day. Why wasn't you picking up?" Animal was watching the news smoking a cigar.

"You heard about what happened at Bulletproof Records today?"

"Yeah, I'm watching it on the news now, but this still ain't answer my question."

"That was me they tried to kill today. My home girl got killed. She died protecting me."

Animal sat up in the chair when she said that. "What the fuck you mean? Who the fuck sending bullets at you like that? And what the fuck Gangster talking about?"

"I think it was Cash. Matter fact, I know it was him, but I'll get into that later. It's a long story, but I need a favor from you,"

"What's the favor? What you need?"

"I need to find out where Cash is at. It's time that motherfucker die. I can't keep ducking bullets."

"Let me see what I can do. Where you at right now?"

"The pink houses, laying low with Gangster right now."

"Okay, give me a few. I'll call you back when I know something."

"Thanks, daddy. I owe you one."

"You know what I want from your ass."

"I got you, nasty."

"Good. Now let me see what I can find out."

"Okay."

Animal hung up the phone and called Cash.

After a few rings he picked up. "Talk to me, Animal."

"Meet me behind Ave Court. We need to talk in private."

"Say less. I'm on my way now."

"I'll see you in a few then." Animal hung up the phone and smiled.

Chapter 17

Cash pulled up in his G-wagon and stepped out smoking a blunt. He looked at Animal as he was leaning against his car smoking a cigar. He walked up to Cash and gave him a pound.

"What's good, fam? Why you have me outside late night and shit?"

"You know if I got you out here this time of night it's for a good reason."

"Real talk, so what you got on your mind homie?"

"A favor for a favor. You know I would never ask but I need you on this one." Cash looked Animal in the eyes and pulled his blunt knowing he don't like favors.

"What you talking about?"

"I know where this nigga Gangster is laying his head down at right now."

"What's the catch?"

"Tasha. I need you to give her a pass."

"You know that bitch set up my little homie, Ray-J and got him bodied, right?"

"Cash, how many mothers, fathers, sisters, brothers, you done had bodied? You know the lifestyle we live. Motherfuckers get bodies all the time. We made it so far in the game because we respect the rules to it."

"I'm give this bitch a pass because I really want Gangster dead, but if she step foot on any of my blocks that bitch is going to be dead dead. Hands down."

"I respect what you are saying. I'll call you tomorrow with the apartment number."

"Animal, you know I have a great deal of respect for you. Right?"

"And you know I have the same respect for you, Cash."

Both of them dapped each other up before going their way. Cash got in the G-wagon and called Big Apple. After a few rings, he picked up.

"Talk to me, Cash. What's the word?"

"I just had a meeting with Animal. He said he will give up Gangster's location if I give the bitch Tasha a pass."

"And what the fuck did you say?"

"I let that genie come out that bottle, but I told his ass if she steps foot on any of our blocks, we are going to roll the bitch."

"Fuck it, you got the addy?"

"I'll get that shit tomorrow when he call my line."

"Copy that. Keep me posted."

"Already." Cash hung up the phone and pulled off smiling because killing Gangster was going to be personal.

***

Animal called Tasha. She picked up after the first ring. She saw Gangster was sleep so she walked into the next room.

"Hey, what's up?"

Animal pulled his cigar before talking. "Are you sure you want to go at Cash?"

"I want to stand over his lifeless body and spit in his face."

"The balls in our court. I got him coming to the pink housing tomorrow. I just need an apartment number to send him to."

"I can get that for you."

"Send it to me then and Tasha don't miss because this shit will fall back on me. So, stand on your business."

"I got this. I'll call you tomorrow morning with the info."

"Cool. I'll be waiting to hear from you." Animal hung up the phone and pulled off.

Chapter 18

Gangster opened his eyes to see Tasha lying next to him. He started kissing on her neck, lightly waking her up.

Tasha rolled over and looked at him. "Baby, I see you are up early."

"Yeah, I am, and so is Mr. Thickness. He needs some love."

"Okay but I have to talk to you about something first."

"Baby I got you but please let me get this nut first."

"Okay come on." Tasha smiled and started sucking on Gangster dick. She was licking all around it. She was deep throating it like a pro as she was holding his balls. Gangster had a big dick but Animal's dick was thicker and longer so sucking Gangster dick wasn't nothing to her no more. Gangster had his hand on her head with his eyes closed. She ain't never suck his dick like this before. She was rotating her hand and tongue all over him. Gangster moaned as he was cumming into her mouth. Tasha had his whole dick in her mouth as her tongue was licking all over his balls. She took his dick out of her mouth and showed him her tongue as she smiled.

"Dam you just did that. That's how you wake a nigga up in the morning. Facts."

"You know I got you, daddy."

"Already, sexy. So, what you want to talk to me about?"

"I found a way to get Cash killed."

Gangster sat up in the bed and looked at Tasha.

"How?"

"My homegirl Tonya said Cash been trying to fuck her. He think she lives over here, so I can get her to set him up for us, bae."

"Can you trust her?"

"Yeah, I can."

"Good. Set it up. We will use this spot to body him in. Go let your people know it's a go and I'ma move all this shit to the other spot."

"Okay. I'm going to do that now."

"Facts. Go handle the business."

Tasha got up and walked out of the room to the shower. Gangster got dressed and called Savage. Savage picked up after a few rings.

"What's the word, big homie?"

"I need you at the Pinks. We are about to put Cash in a fucking grave."

"I'm on my fucking way. You just made my day."

"Well hurry up and get here so we can stand on this business."

"Say less." Gangster hung up the phone and did a line of coke as he waited for Savage to get over there.

***

Cash looked around at everyone in the warehouse as he loaded his gun up.

"In a little while we are all headed to the pink houses. I found out that Gangster been ducked off over there. We ain't doing no talking when we pull up. Kado, you and Soulja are with each other. I want y'all to come from the back. Rip and Symone y'all post up in the front. If you see Gangster, you kill Gangster. Me and Big Apple are walking into the projects. It's time we lay this bitch ass nigga down to rest."

"I want to kill that bitch Tasha so bad. I hope she with him," Symone said.

Big Apple looked at Cash.

"Symone, don't worry about her. We want Gangster. That's who your bullet need to be shooting at."

Nobody said nothing. They all knew it was go time.

***

"21-B, that's the apartment number. I have everything set up already. We just waiting on Cash to come through."

Animal puffed on his cigar and nodded. "Cool, I'm about to shoot him the info now. You just make sure you come back to me."

"I got you, daddy."

Animal smiled and hung up the phone and called Cash.

Cash picked up on the first ring. "You got the apartment number?"

"Yeah, 21-B and remember our deal."

"I ain't forget, homie. I'ma stand on my word as long as the info you gave me is 100."

"That's nothing to worry about. Just stand on your business and body this nigga."

"Bet." Cash hung up the phone and looked at Big Apple. "Let's go roll this nigga."

"Now that's what the fuck I'm talking about."

Cash did his finger in a circle, letting everyone know it was time as he jumped into his G-wagon.

***

Gangster had the M16 on him. He was in a blue van along with Tasha. Savage was in the park with both Mac-11s on him as they waited for Cash.

"Tasha, I want to kill this nigga so bad my dick is getting hard. I want to see him take his last breath," Gangster said as he had the M16 in his hand looking out the window.

"I know how bad you want him dead. Every time I close my eyes, I see Nicole face as she was getting shot. She died for me. I want him dead just as bad as you." Tasha tapped Gangster's arm when she saw Cash's G-wagon pull up.

"Good, it's showtime. Let's get ready to body this nigga."

Cash stepped out of the G-wagon along with Big Apple.

"Cash, something feels funny about all of this," Big Apple said as he looked around.

"I been knowing Animal for a long time now. If he said he's here, then he's here."

"If he ain't, I'm personally going to put two bullets in his fucking head." Cash and Big Apple walked into the pink houses. Kado looked at Savage in the park with his hoodie on then he looked at the blue van.

"Soulja, Gangster knew we was coming. This is a setup."

"Ain't no way he would know this was a setup."

"I'm telling you look at the nigga in the park and the blue van Cash is walking right in the middle of this shit."

Kado took off running to Cash when Cash saw him. He looked as Savage pulled both Mac-11s out and started shooting them at Cash. Soulja started shooting at Savage. Savage took off shooting as he was running. That's when the van doors opened and Gangster started shooting the M16. Cash ducked down behind a tree and started shooting back. Big Apple was shooting at the van, Tasha put the van in drive headed right at Big Apple. Big Apple jumped out the way before he got hit. Tasha crashed the van into the gate at the park bullets were flying from everywhere. Tasha jumped out the van and Kado looked at her with his gun to her face.

"Yeah bitch, it's time to hear that boom." Before he could pull the trigger, Savage came from the other side and shot Kado all in the back and face with the Mac-11, killing him. Symone and Rip were running to the other side, shooting at Gangster. That's when you heard the sounds of the police coming. Big Apple saw them and started shooting at them along with Soulja. Savage looked around then at Tasha.

"We got to get the fuck out of here now. It's too many of them plus the boys in blue. We are out man and outgunned."

"What about Gangster?"

"He knows how to move. We have to go now."

Tasha went to take off running but she stopped. She pointed her gun at Big Apple and Soulja and started shooting. She shot Soulja in the back, dropping him before she took off running, Gangster was still shooting it out with Symone and Rip. Cash ran to help Soulja up. He had the perfect shot at Gangster, but he let it go to get Soulja off the ground. Gangster took off running. Symone took off behind him. Big Apple shot one of the cops in the neck, killing him. Cash got Soulja to his G-wagon and took off.

"Big bro, we got to get the fuck out of here now." Rip yelled to Big Apple. Both of them took off to Rip cars as bullets was still flying their way. As more police cars were coming on the scene, Rip went to get in the car and was shot two times by the police. Big Apple started shooting back, hitting another cop in the chest and leg dropping him. He got Rip in the car and he peeled off. Going on a high-speed chase with the police, Gangster ran down an alley and stopped to catch his breath when Symone came from behind him and said,

"Yo, we good. We lost them."

Gangster turned around and looked at Symone as she started firing bullets into his chest. Gangster fell to the ground. Symone stood over top of him.

"I fucking hate you. I fucking hate you!" She yelled as she shot him in the face two times, killing him. She ran out the alley and started walking down the street. She waved down a yellow cab and got inside. The streets were flooded with police everywhere. Tasha and Savage made it back to the other apartment. You had the local news stations out there going live. Animal was watching the news with Killer

"Killer, it looks like a fucking war zone out there right now. Dead cops and all," Animal said as he puffed his cigar.

"Yeah, them motherfuckers was standing on business today."

Cash was headed to the warehouse when he looked at Soulja. "You good homie?"

"Yeah, that bitch clapped me, dog." Soulja was bleeding badly.

"You good I'm going to get you some help. Just hang on."

As Cash was pulling up to the warehouse, so was Big Apple. They got Rip and Soulja inside. They was putting pressure on both they gunshot wounds. Cash was on the phone with Alexis.

"Look, I need you at the warehouse now. Both of my niggas are bleeding the fuck out."

"Alright, I'm on my way now." Cash hung up the phone and looked at them.

"Y'all hang in there. Help is on the way."

Big Apple walked up to Cash. "I don't give a fuck about what you say. Animal is a fucking dead man now. That whole shit was a fucking set up. Kado is dead, Rip is shot. Soulja is shot and we don't even know what happened to Symone. I told you we couldn't trust that nigga"

"I'ma deal with it alright, Apple."

"No, I'm going to fucking deal with this nigga."

Big Apple and Cash looked as the warehouse doors opened up and Symone walked in side up to them.

"Damn I'm glad you good. What the fuck happened to you?"

Gangster took off running and I took off behind him, Cash."

"So, where this nigga at now?" Big Apple asked

"Dead. I emptied the clip in that nigga chest and face. He's fucking dead dead." Cash looked at Symone and nodded Big Apple did too.

"Good. Now, we just got one more bridge to burn down," Big Apple said.

"No, two more. That bitch Tasha is still alive and she needs to fucking die yesterday."

That's when Alexis came walking through the door and Cash ran up to her.

Chapter 19

"This is a fucking shit show out here. One dead cop, one dead suspect, and America's Most Wanted Chad Mosly aka Gangster. Somebody wanted him dead," Captain Moore said.

"Gangster still had beef with Browns. This was a gang war. They wanted Gangster dead so now this bullshit might be over."

"Yeah, let's hope so, Detective Cross, because the news is having a field day with this right now."

Both Detective Cross and Captain Moore were looking around at the two local news teams going live on the scene.

***

"Damn, they got the homie. I thought he got the fuck out of there," Savage said as he puffed on his blunt. Tasha was lost for words just watching the news.

"Savage, this all went wrong. How the fuck they get down on us like that?"

"You know Cash ain't going nowhere alone. We should have been more on point, if anything."

"So, what the fuck we going to do now? Like I have some money put to the side, but Cash is still going to be all over our asses."

"Fuck Cash. I'm still flying my green flag. My brother, Jamaica died wearing these colors. I'm flying them for me and him now."

"You right. Nicole died for me too so we are in this to the end. What do you have in mind?"

"I still have all the kilos. I just need to open up shop somewhere and take off from there."

"Yeah, let's do this." Tasha watched the news as they were taken the bodies away. At the end of the day, no matter what, she loved him. He was more than her rock, but he was her Gangster.

***

Animal smoked his cigar, still watching the news.

"I had this shit set up to the tee. How the fuck do they fumble this shit?"

"It looks like World War 3 out there. Vans crashed into gates, bodies everywhere. Dead police. Shit is ugly out there right now."

"Just be on point because Cash might think I set his ass up and we might have to flatline his ass."

"If he knock at this door, I'm body his ass if he try something."

"I already know." Animal picked up his phone and called Tasha. She picked up after the first ring.

"Hey, I was going to call you," Tasha said as she was walking in the other room for privacy.

"Yeah, you should have called me because I see Gangster was rolled last night but Cash is still breathing. Your plan ain't fucking work so that put me on the hot seat because of your fuck up."

"We are going to take care of Cash real soon. This shit ain't over."

"Just handle your business. I did my part, now you do yours."

"I'll call you in a few days when it's done."

"I'll be waiting on your call." Animal pulled his gun out knowing shit was about to go boom.

"Animal, we know how Cash gets down. We need to send Lil Shooter."

"You know what, Killer? You're right. Send the boy at him."

**

"How y'all feeling homies?" Cash asked Rip and Soulja as he was smoking his blunt.

"Man, what the fuck you mean? I thought I was going to fucking die the way them bullets hit my ass," Rip said.

"Word. It's fun shooting them bitches but not getting shot by them. That's a whole other story, Cash," Soulja said.

Cash started laughing at both of them. "Soulja, you was bleeding all over my fucking G-wagon. Nigga you owe me $500 for that detail job. Real talk."

"Nigga I was fucking dying. What the fuck you wanted me to say to myself, self, stop bleeding, you are in Cash G-wagon?"

"I don't give a fuck what you say to yourself. I just know you owe me $500, nigga."

"Whatever Cash, but now that Gangster is dead. What now?"

"We still got two more bodies to bury."

"Who the fuck is still left?" Rip asked.

"That bitch, Tasha and Animal who set me the fuck up."

"Fuck it. If they are on the plate, let's get ready to eat," Soulja said.

Cash just nodded as he pulled his blunt.

Chapter 20

Savage stepped out of the car on Poppin Ave. He seen a few niggas making plays. In his mind, he had something to prove. He was the last real nigga flying the green flag and motherfuckers was going to respect his colors. He walked up to the first motherfucker he seen.

"Yo fam, who is holding the block down?"

"Who the fuck are you pulling up asking questions?

"It's always one motherfucker who want to play tough guy," Savage said to himself.

"What the fuck you mean by that nigga?" Savage pulled his gun out and smacked the dude in the face, dropping him to the ground. He then shot one time in the air. Everyone looked at him.

"I ain't come to the block to talk or make friends. Now, who the fuck is holding the block down before this nigga get a bullet pushing his brains to the back of his fucking head. I ain't going to ask no fucking more. On gang!"

"Yo chill, homie. This this is King block."

"That's all the fuck I wanted to know. Get your ass up, pussy. Got me out here showing off on the fucking block."

The dude got up and walked backwards away from Savage.

"Tell that nigga King I said link up with me. My fucking name is Savage. Let him know I got the pure white gold that's better than pussy for 28 a brick. For anybody else who's trying to get money, link up. I'm at the pink houses."

Savage turned around, walked off to his car, got in and pulled off. Knowing he just made a loud statement that he got the work, and he wasn't to be played with.

***

"Cash, we both know that Animal set us up. I don't know if he's fucking that bitch Tasha or not, but Kado is dead because of that nigga and Soulja and Rip are laid up from getting clapped. It's really just me and you right now. We got Symone working the dope spots. We need to go at Animal right now blazing."

Cash took a sip of his drink then shot the 8 ball in the corner pocket. "I hear you, Big Apple but we have too many homies down right now to go at Animal. Do you really want to go into another war right now? We need to let the smoke clear out of the kitchen before we start blazing a new fire, real talk."

Big Apple just nodded.

"Y'all ready to do this. We ain't doing no talking when we pull up just pop out and bust on these clown ass niggas."

Trap said there were two black SUVs driving back-to-back with the windows rolled down. They pulled up in the front of the pool hall. Big Apple looked then yelled, "Get down." as bullets were flying through the window from five high power assault rifles. The windows were shot out, the bottles on the bar were shot. Glass was flying everywhere. Cash went to run and was shot in the leg, dropping down to the floor. Big Apple was shooting back from behind the bar. Two men ran into the pool hall, Cash hit one in the chest, dropping him. Big Apple shot one in the shoulder, pushing him back out the door. Bullets were still flying then all you heard was the sound of car tires peeling off. Big Apple ran to the pool hall door to see the SUVs turning the corner. He went back into the pool hall and looked at all the broken glass and bullet holes everywhere. He ran to Cash to help him on his feet.

"You good, Cash?"

"Yeah, I got fucking shot but it ricocheted off the floor and hit me. Fuck."

"Well, you killed one of them bitches and I shot one. Gangster dead. He don't have shooters like this. That was some heavy shit they was shooting at us. Fuck what you talking about, Animal just shot first at us."

Cash just looked around at the pool hall at everything that was shot up, knowing Big Apple was right. Animal just opened up pandora's box and he was playing for keeps.

***

Killer walked up to Animal as he was sitting in his chair with 2 stress balls in his hand, smoking his cigar. He looked at Killer.

"I just got word that they shot the pool hall up with over 2000 rounds."

"Is Cash dead?"

"They didn't say but we did lose one of our own and one of them also got shot."

"I see this nigga Cash just don't want to fucking die. Keep our people on point because he is going to come back. How, I don't know, but if anybody from Browns come into this project, they die here."

"Copy. I'll let it be known." Killer walked off as Animal said to himself, "It's time to see who can play chess better, Cash. Me or you."

Chapter 21

Savage was sitting in the park, smoking a blunt when he seen King and two of his goons walking his way. They walked in the park right up to him. Savage got off the bench when they walked up to him.

"I heard you came to my block looking for me, being disrespectful."

"Nah, that's not the story, my guy. I asked nicely then I got on the gangster shit because that's the vibe a motherfucker gave me."

"Well, you were looking for me. I'm in your face now. What business you got to talk to me about?"

"28 a bird. 99% pure. I know you can't beat them prices."

"What makes you think I can't?"

"You wouldn't be standing here if you could. We can play games to see who dick is bigger or we can do business."

"And how I know our shit is 99% pure. I never heard of you, nigga."

"One, I don't play games, and I don't like wasting my fucking time. You are going to hear a lot about me. My name is Savage, the new top dog of Go-Gettas."

"So, you took Gangster place?"

"Just know I'm standing in front of you now with a green flag. Are we going to do business or talk?"

"Let me see what you are working with."

Savage picked up the book bag and threw it to King.

"It's a quarter bird in there, keep it. If you like what I'm working with, you know where to find me. Just know it's 28 a bird. I don't care how many you buy I'm not going under that price."

"Say less. If I'm fucking with it, I will be in touch."

"I'll see you soon then." Savage looked at all 3 of them and walked off.

"Yo, Mickey-B, do a background check on this nigga. Let's find out who the fuck he is and where he getting his work from."

"You know I'm on that shit. I got you, King."

"Good. Now, let's get the fuck out of here." King looked around one more time before walking off.

Savage knew he had them. It was just a waiting game now.

***

Monica walked out of her apartment with Adrian, both of them were wearing matching outfits. They were looking so cute when someone called Monica name. She stopped and saw it was a local hustler named Face. She stopped as he ran up to her.

"Damn Monica, you got your grown and sexy on I see."

"Face, what do you want? I don't have time for your games."

"I'm grown grown. I don't have time for games. Seeing what's up with you? I'm trying to link up with you later."

"That's not going to happen now. If you don't mind, I was on my way to the stone before you stopped me."

"Damn, a bitch gets some new clothes and we don't see her for a few months and she start acting all new and shit. Remember, you are the same bitch that was sucking me and my man's dick for a ten dollar rock."

"You know what? Fuck you, Face and your little dick." Monica turned around and walked off. Face yelled out,

"Don't worry. You will be smoking real soon and I'll be dropping more babies off at that daycare in your stomach, bitch."

Face walked back over to his mans and laughed as he dapped them up. Monica had a tear in her eye just thinking what he said in front of everyone. She ain't want to be at that apartment no more. She just really wanted to move. Adrian looked up at her as she wiped the tears out her eyes.

***

Symone sat back and thought about Gangster. How they used to smoke together, play fight and how he used to have her make runs for him. He always told her that their loyalty is unbreakable. He had her back for life no matter what but all that shit was just game. Cash showed her real loyalty and what a real family was from the very beginning. She hated Gangster and killing him was just the tip of the iceberg. She wanted everything around him dead and Tasha was at the top of her hit list. Her phone went off and she saw it was Big Apple calling her. She picked up.

"Hey, what's up?"

"Come to the warehouse. We need you over here now."

"Cool, I'm on the way." Symone hung up the phone. She knew it was big because Apple never calls her. She knew something was about to go down or it went down already.

Chapter 22

"Captain, do you have a minute?" Captain Moore looked at Detective Cross. She placed her pen down on the desk.

"Sure, come in Detective. What's on your mind?"

"I decided to run the picture on the news about the serial killer. I don't and can't live with myself if another family gets killed and I let it happen.

"Are you sure that's what you want to do?"

"Yes, it is, Captain. I been thinking about it for the last week now."

"Okay. Let's run the story on the news and get his picture in the paper."

"Thank you, Captain."

"No problem, Detective."

Detective Cross walked out of the Captain's office knowing what he just did was the right move. It would be wrong to cause someone else pain just to heal his.

***

"Tasha, you know why I don't like putting my face on shit? Because it puts me in situations like the one I'm in now because of you," Animal said as he looked at Tasha in the parking lot of the old run down warehouse.

"I told you I'm taking care of this. Cash is going to slip up real soon. That's when I'm going to body his ass."

"You know who I bet on when I need to get shit done? I depend on me, Tasha."

"So, you had me come out here tonight so you can chew me up?"

"No, I need you to make a pickup for me. Can you do that for me?"

"Yeah, I can, Animal. Where I'm going?"

"Philly. I already texted you the address. You going to see my man, Jackson. Handle this for me and we will call it even on your fuck up with Cash."

"Cool, I got you."

"Already, sexy." Animal kissed Tasha. Even though she fucked up, he wasn't going to treat her fucked up. He understood everyone fucks up. Nobody is perfect in this life they live by.

***

Symone walked into the spot to see Big Apple loading up two guns. Nobody else was there. Symone walked up to Big Apple.

"Hey, what's up? Where everyone at?"

"Cash was shot in the leg last night. Rip and Soulja I sent them to take your spot at the trap spot tonight. We have to go get our hands bloody. All I need you to do is drive and I'm going to take care of the rest."

"Shit I'm ready to ride, let's go put that work in."

Big Apple smiled when she said that. "Good because we are hitting up one of Animal spots where he keep most of his shit at."

"How you found out where his spot is at?" Big Apple pointed to the far end of the warehouse where there was a chair, and a man tied down to it. Symone ain't even see him when she walked into the warehouse.

"Who the fuck is that?"

"One of Animal shooters. I thought Cash killed him but he hit him in the chest. He fell backwards, hitting his head on the floor, knocking him out cold. We had a long talk with him last night and he told me everything I needed to know."

"How did you get him to talk?" Big Apple smiled then took the cup that was on the table and flipped it upside down, dropping all his bloody teeth on the table along with two fingers.

"I have my ways. He just needed a little convincing. That's all."

"Damn. Well fuck it, let's do this." Big Apple handed Symone a gun as they walked out the warehouse.

***

"Big Apple, his main spot is a deli where he keep all his shit at."

"It's really smart. It's in the open around everyone and nobody knows. You see the car over there to the right?"

"Yeah, I see it."

"Those niggas are his watch dogs. Look, keep the car running while I go take care of the business."

"Say less. If you need me, I'm coming."

"Trust me, I'm the real Animal in these streets." Big Apple stepped out of the car and put his hoodie on.

He walked behind the deli. The car door opened, and both dudes got out, holding their guns in their hand. They walked on the side of the deli. As soon as they reached the back of the deli, Big Apple swung his knife and slit one of their throat. He chopped the other one in the neck making him lose his breath. He then walked up to him and jammed his knife in his throat, killing him making him choke on his own blood. He wiped the knife down on the dude shirt and pulled their bodies out of sight. He then looked around and picked the deli lock, opening the back door. Going inside, he looked around and made it to the back room. That's where he saw boxes of money. More than he could fit in the car. He pulled his phone out and called Symone. She picked up on the first ring.

"Hey, what's up? You need me to come back there?"

"No, look. Go get the van now, and hurry up, move fast."

"Okay, I'm going now."

Big Apple hung up the phone and looked around some more. He found a few kilos of cocaine. He looked at his watch, waiting on Symone to come back so they can move all this shit.

***

"King, this little nigga shit is A1. It's everything he said it was."

"So, you telling me it's better than the shit we have already?"

"Yeah, much better."

King puffed his blunt thinking to himself

"So, you know what Nate? Why the fuck I'ma pay this little nigga for something I can just take?"

"Shit, a 187 and a come up. That sounds like a win win to me. When you trying to roll this nigga and get the pack?"

"Set that shit up for tomorrow night. Let his ass know we want 20 and if he ain't got 20, we will take what he has."

"Shit, I'm about to head over there right now."

"Good, go stand on that business and let me know what he say."

"Say less, King. I'll hit you back in a few."

King watched as Nate went to stand on his business, putting his gun on his waist and walking out the front door.

"Symone look, move fast. We already been here an hour too long."

Big Apple stressed to Symone as they were loading up the van.

"Damn, how much money you think is in there?"

"A few Ms at the most. Animal been doing this for years. His father, father was the plug now he is. Come on, we have two more boxes then we getting the fuck out of here."

Big Apple grabbed one box then Symone grabbed the other one. As they made their way to the van, Big Apple saw two cars pull up.

"Fuck, you got your hammer on you, right?"

"Hell yeah."

"Good because it's about to go down."

The dudes got out of the car, guns in hand. That's when two police cars came riding down the street. They saw the guns and put they lights on. All you heard was, "Freeze, drop your weapons." then gunshots going off.

"Symone, get the box in the van so we can get the fuck out of here, now."

Symone threw the box in the van and Big Apple pulled out from the back of the deli, cutting through the alley as Animal men was having a shootout with the police. As they was driving, you saw more police cars headed their way to the deli.

"Symone, now that's a great escape."

"Who the fuck you telling? I just knew we was going to go out blazing."

"Me too, but tonight Animal just took a mean fucking blow."

"And we just got a mean come up."

"Fucking right. Call Cash and tell him to meet us at the spot now."

Symone pulled her phone out and did what Big Apple told her to do.

Chapter 23

"Animal, it's ugly as fuck right now. We have three dead shooters and both our guards are dead. The deli's been hit. There's no money or work in there." Animal kicked over the table and pointed at Killer.

"How the fuck did anybody know about that spot? All my shit is fucking gone."

"Yeah, everything." Animal sat down for a second before he jumped up yelling in a state of rage.

"Killer, find out how they knew about my spot, and who had enough heart to try me like this. I want they whole fucking family dead."

"I think we should be going at Cash. That's the only person we got smoke with right now."

"Hit the block and tell me what you find out so these bodies can start dropping."

"I'm on it now, boss." Animal pulled his cigar and bit it in a sign of stress.

***

"Look, I don't know nigga, but you have heart. I respect that. I respect how you pulled up on the block. Let me tell you something, King ain't holding like that. His work is 70% pure if that. If he was holding like that, he would have never pulled up on you. Watch your back with him is all I'm saying."

"My thing is why you telling me this? Ain't that your man. Don't you work for him?"

"I'm trying to eat and he is the only one fucking with the block right now."

"You did some real shit putting me on game. If shit is what you say it is, I'm going to hit you up. I need some real motherfuckers flying my colors and getting this money with me. You down to wear that green flag?"

"Hell yeah, I'm down to wear that flag and get that cake."

"Say no more then. Just know, everybody get blood on they hands before that green flag go on the right side."

"Nigga I'm down. Just let me know when and where."

"I got you." Savage dapped Ant up before he walked off. If shit was what Ant said it was, he was going to body King and take his blocks over on a real power move.

***

"I know this motherfucker is tight right now. Yo, Big Apple you really are a fucking bulldog in these streets and I see you bring the little bulldog with you. Just by eyeballing this bread it looks like a good five million. Plus, 15 bricks. What you going to do with the body in the back?" Cash asked as he smoked on his blunt.

"By now, this motherfucker want to know who hit him. We ain't going to throw a rock and hide our hand. I'ma drop the nigga body off to him and all his teeth I pulled out and two fingers I cut off."

Symone was smoking a Newport as they was talking.

"Look, have Soulja and Rip help Symone move all of this to the other warehouse. You do what you do with that body. I'ma drop them 15 kilos off to the other trap then I have to go pull up on Monica. She called me last night, but I missed her call. I was on the phone with Symone"

"Cool, go take care of your business. Hit me up when you are done."

"Copy that." Cash gave Big Apple a pound before walking off into his G-wagon with the 15 kilos of cocaine.

***

K-9 walked up to Tasha, as she stood there looking sexy as hell. His men were loading up the van for her.

"So, how long have you been working for Animal?"

"I don't work for Animal. We just have an understanding with each other."

"A lady that speaks her mind respectfully. I was under the impression that you worked for Animal. He told me how loyal and trustworthy you are. I heard about the last run you did for him. It ain't end too well for two people"

"They made they bed and I put them in there for good. I stand on business no matter who I'm dealing with."

"Maybe one day me and you can do business."

"You have to take that up with Animal. I don't know you and right now I'm working with him respectfully."

"I respect that and that's good to know that you are honest and stand on your business because let me tell you something you might not know."

"And what's that?"

K-9 walked a little closer to Tasha and said, "Animal works for me, sweetheart." K-9 walked out the back of the van after saying that and closed the doors.

"You are all loaded up. I know how to reach you. Drive safe, I'll see you soon."

Tasha ain't say a word. She got in the van and before she pulled off, her phone got a text that said K-9. She turned her head and looked at him. He winked at her before she pulled off, knowing she was just talking to the top dog.

***

The black Range Rover pulled up on the block. Cash stepped out of it and looked at all the dudes standing around. He ain't say nothing to them as he walked to Monica apartment on his cane. He opened the door and went inside. Adrian ran up to him and gave him a hug. He picked her up and kissed her on the forehead.

"Hey little angel, where is your mother at?"

"She in the bathroom, taking a shower."

Before Cash could say another word, Monica came out the bathroom dripping wet with a towel over her body, walking up to Cash and Adrian.

"Hey, Cash, you just got here?"

"Yeah, I just walked through the door and baby girl ran and jumped on me."

"Well, I hope baby girl got her room clean like I asked her to an hour ago or should I go look to see for myself."

"I'm going to do it now, mom. I will see you later, Cash." Adrian ran off to her room.

"Cash, let me go put something on. I'll be right back."

"Cool. I'll be right here waiting on you." Monica walked off to get dressed. Cash was proud of her knowing she was keeping her word to him and her daughter.

***

"Savage, what's the word?" Nate said as he walked up to him.

"Just chasing paper, what's good though?"

They gave each other a pound.

"King told me to pull up on you. He's trying to get 20 of them birds you was talking about."

"Oh word, yeah let's set that up. When is he trying to bust that move?"

"Tonight. What's a good time?"

"Pull up at 9. All stacks of 1000. It's easier for me to count that way and I ain't with 30 motherfuckers pulling up to my spot. You and him. Let me make that real fucking clear from the jump."

"I'll let him know."

"Good." Savage handed Nate his number before walking off.

***

"So, what's up, Monica? You called me last night. My bad I missed your call."

"It's okay. It was just some bullshit. I ain't worried about it no more."

"Well, tell me about this bullshit. I want to know."

With a deep breath Monica said, "This dude I used to trick with name Face just been coming out his face to me. Yesterday, he did it when I had Adrian with me going to the store. I'm just thinking maybe it's time for me to move from over here and start off someplace new."

"No. We don't run from our problems. We deal with them. Show me this dude Face right now."

"Cash."

"What I just say?" Monica got up and walked out the front door with Cash. She looked at the guys standing on the steps. "He's the one with the gray hoodie on."

"Stay right right here." Cash walked over to the guys with his cane. Everyone looked at him when he walked up.

"Face, I see you have a mouth problem. So, you know what? How about I shut that bitch permanently for you, nigga."

"Cash, I respect who you are but you pulling up on me about a recovering crackhead. What part of the game is that?"

"I don't like repeating myself so this is what I'm going to do because a nigga like you have to learn the hard way."

"What the fuck you mean by that?" Face stood up when he said that.

"I got two kilos on this pussy nigga head to the first motherfucker that body this bitch."

Face looked around and saw one of the dudes pulling his gun out. He punched the dude in the face and took off running. Cash watched as they started shooting at him.

Cash yelled out, "I want proof of kill," as everyone took off after him. He turned around and looked at Monica as he walked up to her.

"I'll find you a new place this week to move into."

"Okay, thank you."

"No problem. I have some shit to go take care of. I'll be back tomorrow to check on you."

"Okay."

Cash walked to his Range Rover and got inside. He looked at Monica one more time and pulled off.

Chapter 24

Killer walked to his car and looked and saw all the bloody teeth on his windshield wiper along with his two fingers. He looked in his car and saw one of his shooter's dead body in the backseat. He looked around at the dark parking lot in the project. He took a rag and picked up all the teeth and two fingers. He opened up the trunk of his car, pulled an old jacket out and threw it over the body. He got into his car and drove off, knowing he had to dump the body somewhere. Now, he knew who hit them. One name, one word. Cash. He pulled his phone out and called Animal. After a few rings, Animal picked up.

"What you got for me, Killer?"

"A dead body."

"What the fuck you mean a dead body?"

"I came to my fucking car and there is a dead body in the backseat, missing all his teeth and two fingers."

"Do you recognize him?"

"Yeah, he's one of our shooters we sent at Cash. Now, we know who hit us up because they did a number on this motherfucker,"

"Yeah, so what are you about to do?"

"Dump this body off, burn this car and be on my way back to you."

"Say less. I'll be here when you get back."

"Copy that." Animal hung up the phone and called Cash.

Cash looked at the number and laughed as he picked up the phone.

"You got some heart calling me. Nigga what the fuck you want?"

"What the fuck I want? How about my money and dope back nigga?"

"You sound dumb as fuck right now. Suck dick, nigga."

"I'm about to send 100 rounds at your fucking head."

"You did and you missed, nigga. Twice but when my shooters come, we hit the bullseyes. Pussy keep your vest on nigga because we coming straight at you."

Animal ain't say nothing. He hung up the phone, lit his cigar, looked out the window and said to himself, "Silence is the best reply to a dead man walking." With a smile on his face

Savage watched as King and Nate walked into the projects with a book bag over their shoulders. Savage walked up to them.

"Let's do business now that you are here."

"That's money and work up front. So, you got the work?"

"Yeah, come on." Savage walked them to the empty apartment where there was one table with two duffle bags on it. Savage walked to the table, picked up one kilo of cocaine and threw it at King.

King caught it. "Yeah, this shit looks good. Let's see what's it's hitting on though." King passed it to Nate. Nate took a knife, opened it up and sniffed some of it off the tip of the knife.

"Yeah King, that's that guy. This shit is hitting."

"Now that you see that I came through on my end, let me see that cake."

"Yeah, let me give you that bread." King threw Savage the book bag on the floor and so did Nate. When Savage picked the bag up, Nate pulled his gun out on him and so did King.

"This how the fuck y'all playing the game?"

"What the fuck you thought we was going to pay for this shit, nigga? We block boys. Now, run all this shit nigga," King said.

Savage stood up. "Cool, I see how y'all are trying to get down on me."

"You know the rules to this game, nigga. You fucked up and got caught slipping."

"Everybody fumbles the ball just know that, King."

"Yeah but too bad you won't be able to see it, because pussy nigga you die tonight."

That's when the room door opened up and Ant came out blasting a Glock-45, hitting Nate in the neck, dropping him. King looked at Nate on the floor coughing up blood. Savage pulled his gun out and pointed it at King's head.

"Yeah, pussy nigga, what was you saying now?"

"What the fuck you going to do now, nigga? I ain't copping no pleas."

"Good, motherfucker just die." Savage pulled the trigger, shooting King in the head. His body fell down right next to Nate. Savage looked at both of them lying in pools of blood.

"You was on point. Both of them pussy niggas was trying to set me up."

"I told you them niggas dirty. Hands down."

"You fucking right you did. Let's see what they got in them book bags." Savage opened up a book bag and laughed when he seen crumpled up paper inside. "Them niggas was dirty as fuck."

"I told you."

Savage walked to the table and picked up the duffle bags as Ant picked up the kilo that was on the floor and walked out of the apartment with Savage.

***

"Tasha, how did that run go?" Tasha passed Animal the keys to the van.

"It went smooth. Everything is where it's supposed to be."

"While you were gone, one of my spots was hit for a few million."

Tasha couldn't believe what she was hearing. "Who the fuck did that?" Animal pulled his cigar before talking, "The nigga you was supposed to kill. Cash. You see how your fuck up cost me money."

"Look, somebody put him on point. He was ready guns blazing."

"Don't worry you going to make it right."

"You said this would make us good if I do this run for you, Animal."

Animal smiled as he puffed his cigar, "That was before I lost 4 million dollars. Like I said you going to help me make it right. I'll call you in a few days."

"Yeah, do that." Tasha walked off shaking her head. She picked her phone up and called Savage. He picked up after a few rings.

"Where the fuck you been? I been blowing your damn phone up for two days now."

"I had to go out of town and take care some business. It's along fucking story."

"You think you have a story. Niggas just tried to roll me last night. I need you to pull up to the old spot like ASAP."

"I'll be there in 20 minutes."

"Cool." Savage hung up the phone and lit his blunt as he finished watching the game.

Chapter 25

Cash waited under the bridge off of Grint Street in front of his G-wagon. He smoked his blunt, waiting on Smash and Solo to pull up with proof of kill. That's when he saw the black Ford pull up and both of them stepped out the car with a bookbag in Solo hand.

"What's good, Cash?"

"You know me getting money and running shit."

"Trust me, I know how you move already. That's why we bring you this."

"Let me see what you have for me."

Solo opened up the book bag and showed Cash Face's head in the bag. "You asked for proof of kill. It don't get no more clear then this, baby."

"Hungry wolves. That's what the fuck I'm talking about. I need niggas like you working with me." Cash puffed his blunt, walked to the backseat of the truck and picked up a bag to bring back to Solo.

"Check that out, baby boy. What you know about that?"

Solo smiled and passed the bag to Smash who started smiling when he looked inside.

"99%. That shit is better than pussy. Y'all got my math. Link up and I'll put you in one of my spots."

"Say less Cash, we on it."

"Good and get rid of that. Put it with the nigga's body so his mother could bury her fucking son."

"We got you, big bro."

Cash nodded, walked back to his G-wagon, got inside and drove off.

***

Killer walked up to Animal and placed the rag with the bloody teeth and two fingers down on the table.

"This was waiting on me when I got to my car with a body in the backseat"

"Where you dump the body at?"

"The East river, and I burned the car."

"Cool. Tasha got the van back to us. I need you to find out where Cash is at. I want you to send all guns at him. I want that motherfucker dead."

"I'll let you know when I know something."

"Good because this shit is personal."

"I already know." Killer walked off, knowing he had a job to do. Animal wasn't Gangster and Cash was going to find that out the hard way.

***

Savage pulled up on the block with Ant in the car. He pulled his gun out to make sure he had one in the head. Then, he looked at Ant.

"You ready to do this?"

"Fucking right."

Savage stepped out of the car along with Ant and looked at everyone standing around.

"I'm say this as simple as fuck. King or Nate ain't coming back. So, if y'all niggas want to eat, you need to pull up on me."

One of the dudes walked up on Savage.

"And who the fuck are you?"

Savage got in his face.

"The new head nigga in charge motherfucker. That's who the fuck I am, so if you want some grade A dope and more cake in your pocket, let's eat. If not, we can let these bullets fly, homeboy. What's rocking what you want to do?"

L's looked around at everyone then said, "Let's get this cake."

"That's what the fuck I'm talking about, baby. Yo Ant, give these niggas a pack and a green flag. We doing this the Go-Getta way." Ant dapped Savage up before he got back in his car and drove off.

**

"This is crazy. They saying in the newspaper that this is the worst year New York City seen on a death toll in over 20 years," Soulja said as he was reading the newspaper. Big Apple looked at him then the back of the newspaper.

"What's the back of the newspaper talking about?" Soulja flipped the newspaper over.

"They talking about that serial killer. They got a blurry ass picture of him up, but you can't see his face, just his hand."

"Let me see."

Soulja handed the newspaper to Big Apple as he looked at the picture in the paper.

"It was pointless to put this picture in the paper. They just gave him more motivation to kill again." He passed the paper back to Soulja.

"Yeah, that is the truth. This is a sick motherfucker doing all these crazy ass killings."

"You at a 100% yet?"

"Yeah, me and Rip are ready to go."

"Good. You back at the trap and Rip is shooting again. We got too much work that we need to move now. I need y'all both on your A game."

"Shit let's run it. Any word from Test?"

"Yeah, Symone been going to check on him. He good. He will be home in a few weeks doing runs again."

"So, when am I going back to the trap?"

"Tomorrow. Make sure Rip is here with you. I got some shit to do. I'll get up with you tomorrow." Big Apple dapped Soulja up before walking away

Chapter 26

"Tasha, real talk, we need to dead this beef with Cash. I just took over King blocks and I got about 20 motherfuckers wearing green flags now. They working on the block for me and I still have 38 kilos of cocaine I need to get off. I can't do that with bullets flying." Tasha looked at Savage as if he was crazy.

"You hear how the fuck you sound? This nigga had Gangster killed. Jamaica and Nicole. All of them are six feet deep because Cash sent shooters their way. Now, you talking about some peace shit."

"I ain't tucking my fucking tail but we ain't ready to go at Cash right now. Gangster tried that shit and everybody got put in a black bag. I just need some time right now. That's all the fuck I'm saying."

"I can't believe the shit that's coming out your mouth, Savage but you know what, I got my own bullshit to deal with. Do what the fuck you need to do. Just know he got a bullet gift wrapped with my name on it."

"I'm take care of all that shit, Tasha."

"Yeah, let's see how this shit plays out Savage, because one thing I know about Cash is the only recipe he has for his opps is a fucking bullet. Gangster, Nicole, and Jamaica is fucking proof of that and guess what fam you are a fucking opp." Tasha just shook her head, turned around and walked off, leaving Savage in his thoughts.

***

"Animal, how we looking?" It's been a week and I ain't heard from you. I asked myself. Did your driver deliver or was there a bump in the road that you ain't tell me about?" K-9 said as he sipped on some Gin and Juice.

"No, there wasn't no bump in the road. Just a little problem that I'm dealing with. I'll have your money to you soon." Animal smoked his cigar, looking out the window after making that statement.

"Your problem is your problem, so don't make it my problem. 72 hours, have my money. Call me when it's on the way and one more thing, I'm taxing you 100K for the late fee." K-9 hung up the phone. K-9 knew Animal's father for years before he was killed but knowing his father ain't give him a pass. And doing business with him don't make them friends is something he told Animal when he stepped into his father's footsteps. If it don't make money, or ain't a business, it's a fucking hobby and he needed all his fucking money.

***

"Mr. Howard, some things you need to keep to yourself. It's not always good to be a helping hand. One thing I know about the police, they don't give a fuck about you. You will just be another dead body on a cold case and they will go about their day like they never knew you."

John Howard sat in the chair, duct taped down sweating out of fear. He had a knife running along his shoulder blade with blood dripping down his chin from the cut on his cheek.

"Since you want to record everything and send it to Detective Cross, let's see how he likes this video we going to send him."

John Howard tried to say something but couldn't because his mouth was covered with tape. John's eyes opened wide. He felt the knife go in his throat and felt his own warm blood coming out of his neck, seconds before he died. They took the bloody knife and wiped it off on John's shirt and wrote Detective Cross name in blood on the wall. He cut out all the lights in the house, turned the recording off and walked out the back door as if he never was there.

***

Mac-Ru looked at Savage as he leaned against his Lexus smoking a blunt.

"So, you took over for Gangster?"

"Everybody is dead but me. I'm the last goon standing but I'm here because I want to keep doing business with you. But for me to do that, I need a favor."

"Let me break it down to you like this, homie. I don't get out my bed unless it's 20 or more kilos and I don't do favors."

"Last time we picked up, we grabbed 40 kilos. I still want that number, but I can't get that number unless you help me out."

Mac-Ru smiled. "And how the fuck can I help you out?"

"You can't get money and beef with niggas. I got a few blocks on smash with niggas working for me, but I'm beefing with Cash so I'm trying to set something up where me and Cash can talk and dead this beef we have with each other."

"I hear you but what you need from me?"

"I need a number for him or someone to set up a meeting for me, somewhere in the open, where we don't have to worry about bullets flying at each other."

"I ain't going to set no meeting up because if shit go wrong that's going to fall back on me. Let me see what I can do. I might be able to get you his math. Give me a few hours to work my ones and twos homie, and if I do this, you better keep your word."

"Mac-Ru, there's two things I have my word and my balls and I don't break them for anyone."

Mac-Ru nodded as he walked back to his car. Savage got into his car and pulled off, knowing he just made good on Cash number.

***

Cash looked at everyone in the room. He puffed on his blunt before talking.

"Nobody in this room is bigger than Browns. Nobody is bigger than the set. We all put work in. We all bleed for Browns or kill for Browns. On that wall over there is all the homies we lost. They are gone but not forgotten. As y'all can see, we got Test back. Baby boy was hit with 7 shells and laid up in the hospital. A little under a year now, he's back ready to hit the block with us running. That's a real fucking goon. We took over all the Go-Getta blocks. They are now my blocks, but y'all know how this street life go, when you kill one beast, there's always another one stepping up. This motherfucker calls himself Animal. He sent shots our way, and we sent bullets flying his way. Shit, we up on that pussy. We got 3 bodies on his bitch ass and a few million, but that don't mean shit to me because I want that pussy nigga head on the chopping block."

Rip yelled out, "So where can we find this pussy ass nigga?"

"Red Hook Project. He runs them bitches. He sees everything that runs in and out of them so this is what we going to do. Soulja, you and Symone going to watch the projects to clock Animal movements, so we know what time he comes and go."

Soulja and Symone nodded at Cash.

"Rip, you and Test are at the trap. I still need all the money coming in from them blocks. My two new all-stars, Smash and Solo, I need you two guarding the trap spot.

Motherfuckers don't know your face and that's good. Me and Big Apple have some personal shit to take care of. Y'all all just stay on point because when it's time to pop that bottle, we ain't doing no talking. We cleaning house." Cash looked at everyone and nodded before him and Big Apple got into his G-wagon and pulled off.

Chapter 27

Savage seen that his phone was ringing. He picked it up to see that Mac-Ru was calling him.

"Mac-Ru, tell me something good."

"I got that number you asked for. You ain't get it from me. Stand on your business and keep your word."

"I thought we had this conversation about my word already and I always stand on my business."

"Yeah, we did. I'm texting you the number now."

Mac-Ru hung up the phone. Savage seen the number come to his phone. He puffed on his blunt and called Cash. After a few seconds, Cash picked up.

"Who is this?" Cash asked as he was watching the football game.

"Savage."

"I don't know no Savage, how you get my number?"

"Look, Gangster dead. I took over the set. I'm just trying to dead whatever beef you have with the Go-Gettas."

Cash sat up when Savage said that. "Who the fuck is this again?"

"Savage."

"Nigga, you need to come see me personally."

"Cool, somewhere open. Where you want to meet at?"

"Central Park in one hour. Come by yourself. If you got my number, then you know how the fuck I look. I'll see you there." Cash hung up the phone, grabbed his gun and walked out the door.

***

"Detective Cross, this came in the mail for you today." Officer Stacy handed him the package

"Thank you, Stacy."

"No problem, Detective." Stacy walked out the office as Detective Cross opened the package and saw the SD card inside. He pulled it out and placed it inside of his laptop. That's when he seen pictures of John Howard on family trips fishing and laughing around a campfire. Then, the screen went black. When it cut back on, you seen John Howard with a knife running across his face then a slash of the knife coming down the right side of his cheek. Detective Cross couldn't believe what he was seeing. Right before he jumped up, Detective Cross seen the knife get jammed into John Howard neck as he bled out. Then, they threw the newspaper on his lap with the picture on the front page.

"Fuck! Fuck! Fuck!" Detective Cross said as he got up and took his laptop to Captain Moore's office, knowing it was because of him running the story that John Howard was murdered.

***

Cash smiled when he seen the gray Lexus pull up. He knew right then and there who Savage was. He puffed on his cigar as Savage walked up to him wearing a green and black hoodie with a pair of black jeans and green Timberland boots.

"So, you running the set now?"

"Yeah, I'm running the hood now."

Cash just nodded when he said that. "But you know we have unfinished business, right? Debt that need to be paid. Bodies that we need to collect on."

"Cash, I ain't trying to beef with you. I got the hood now. I'm just trying to dead this shit. Gangster dead, Showtime dead and a whole lot of motherfuckers who use to fly these colors. You won. How many more bodies you trying to collect?"

"You know how many of my homies are dead because of Gangster. How many of my dogs he done set up and rolled? Just looking at you with them colors on make me want to flatline your ass."

"And how many of his homies your crew done killed? The only thing we are doing is dropping bodies and giving the police a reason to fuck with us."

Cash knew what Savage was saying was right.

"Let me make this real clear to you. All Gangster's old blocks are mine now. I don't want to see your colors or none of your niggas on my blocks. Tasha, that bitch is on thin ice with me. Keep her in line or she will be the first body I collect. This right here is a warning and you only get one. Savage your crew been flying to close to the sun and I am the motherfucking sun. You get what the fuck I'm saying?"

"Yeah, I do."

"Good. See you around, little nigga." Cash walked back to his G-wagon.

Savage watched as he got inside. Savage knew they wasn't ready to go up against Cash but he also knew that sometimes you win even when you lose. He might have lost his old blocks, but he gained a plug and a whole new crew with better blocks for him to run. In his mind, he still won.

Chapter 28

"Symone heads up, ain't that Animal and a few of his goons right there?" Symone leaned up in the car seat and looked.

"Hell yeah that's him, and you see the duffle bag that one guy is carrying? I bet you that money in that bag."

"You know it is already. Look how deep they are. The question is where are they going?"

"It's only one way to find out. Let's follow them."

"Symone just make sure you have your gun out because if they spot us, it's going to be an all-out shootout." Soulja started up the car and started following them.

"Animal what are we going to do about Cash? He act like he can't be stopped. He took over all the old Go-Gettas blocks. He is now flying they colors over there, tagging the streets signs and buildings."

"Cash is a fucking fly on the wall. I can't wait to stand over his body and shoot him in the fucking head. His hourglass is running out of sand as we speak."

'But he got four million dollars of our money and he killed three of our guys. In his mind, he's winning right now."

"Killer, we deal with gun trades, cocaine, kilos of cocaine let me make that clear. We are dealing with made men. Let Cash take over street corners and blocks. That $4 million is just a penny to our dollar. His time is coming. I promise you that."

Killer nodded.

"So, are we making this run or the girl?"

"I think it's time we go see K-9 face to face. It's been a few years since we been in his presence."

"Oh, this should be funny."

Symone pulled out her phone. "Soulja, I have to call Cash. Animal is leaving the city, and I don't know if he still want us to follow him."

"Yeah, you right. Go ahead and make that call. Let's hear what he has to say."

Symone called Cash. He picked up after a few rings.

"Talk to me. What y'all seeing over there?"

"We ain't even at Red Hook no more. We been following Animal for the last hour. He's leaving the city and he have a crew of bodyguards with him, and one of them are carrying a duffle bag."

"Yeah, keep following him. Let's see where he's headed."

"Say less. We on it." Symone hung up the phone and looked at Soulja.

"He said keep following him."

"Fuck it. Let's do this."

***

Monica looked around at her new spot. It was away from the hood and much bigger than her last spot. Cash even went out his way and got Adrian a puppy. Monica sat down and finished watching the movers put everything into her new spot. She looked at Adrian as she was playing with her puppy.

"Adrian baby, mommy will be right back. Let me go pay the movers, okay."

"Okay, mommy."

Monica walked out of her apartment to the front to go pay the movers as they was standing next to they truck.

"Hey, thank y'all so much."

"No problem, ma'am." Monica was handing them the money when she saw Tasha walking into the building. She remembered her from a party that Ray-J brung her to one night when she was with B-God. She paid the movers and walked back into the building. By the time she made it back in there, Tasha was gone but the elevator stopped on the 6th floor. She made it back to her apartment and looked around again smiling. She was grateful to have someone like Cash in her life.

***

Savage pulled up on the block and stepped out the car with his gun in his hand as he walked up to Ant.

"What the fuck is going on out here that I got to pull up on the block, Ant?"

"You got this motherfucker right here saying he ain't eating."

Savage looked at him with an ice-cold grill.

"How the fuck you ain't eating? I put the pack in your hand my fucking self, nigga."

"We serving crackheads on the block while this nigga serving the weight. This nigga the one eating."

"You talking crazy like your fucking jaw is broke nigga. This is my fucking right hand man. My ace. Nigga don't ever compare yourself to him. Was you there busting your fucking gun. Did you body anybody for the set yet? You know what pay me my money, nigga."

"I don't have it all on me yet."

"What the fuck you mean you don't have my money?"

"I'll have that shit by the end of the day."

"Nigga, run what the fuck you got now. Come up off all that shit, pussy."

Ice looked around and reached in his pocket and gave Savage $600. "That's $600 right there."

"Nigga you shorter than a leprechaun dick, and you out here starting shit on my block. Nigga run your chain, your watch, your earrings, your J's. I want all that shit. Come the fuck off all that shit before I catch a body."

Ant pulled his gun out.

Ice shook his head and came off everything. Savage walked up on him.

"You ain't a dope boy no more. You are a lookout now. You got to earn your right to be back on the block and if you ready to drop your flag, let me know. There's only one way out this shit and your ticket is right here in the chamber of my gun."

"No, we ain't got no problem."

"Good. Ant put that nigga in a lookout window now."

"Copy that."

Savage got back in his car and drove off, knowing he had to rule his block with an iron fist.

***

"Cross, you ain't know he was going to come back after John. Nobody did. This is not on you. This is a sick son of a bitch who is sick in the fucking head. We are going to get his ass I promise you that."

Detective Cross looked at John Howard's dead body still tied down to the chair.

"No Captain, I'm telling you now. This ain't no case that's going to make it to the courthouse. I'm going to kill this motherfucker. You can have my gun and badge now, but the next crime scene you come to is going to be his dead fucking body."

Detective Cross walked out the house and looked at all the people standing around to see if he can see his face. He walked to his car and took a sip of Brandy he had in his glove box before pulling off.

Chapter 29

120

"We are way in Philly, Symone. Who the fuck do this nigga Animal know why out here?"

"Somebody very important, Soulja and very dangerous."

Soulja and Symone watched as Animal got out the SUV along with both his bodyguards and Killer. He looked around before going into the auto part shop where three guys that walked him into the shop. Once into the shop, Animal walked up on K-9. His bodyguard passed K-9's bodyguard the duffle bag.

"I see you came and made the drop off personally. How long has it been since we seen each other face to face? 10-12 years?"

Animal pulled out a cigar and passed it to K-9. Then, he pulled out another one, lowered his head and lit it before talking. "It's been 13 years on the head. Plus, from our last phone conversation I thought it might be good to see each other again."

"I guess you ain't like the tone of our last conversation I had."

"K-9, my father told me something before he was killed."

"And what did Beast tell you, Animal?"

"A predator eats what he kills and sometimes they eat the young. See K-9, you feed a bear to keep it from killing you because a hungry bear will turn on you. I learned to be a fucking predator."

"And what's the point of this story down memory lane?"

"I have murdered for you. I have extorted for you. I have dealt with the corruption of the NYPD for you, but the last conversation we had over the phone was you poking the bear, K-9."

"Animal, when you are knee deep in this lifestyle, everyone pokes the bear. Now, let me tell you a little story that you might not know. 18 years ago, Beast's treachery got out of hand. He was a victim of his own ice cold karma. I called him into this very shop you are standing in right now and I told him the domino effect threatens all of us behind his actions. He was putting all of us in a fucked up predicament but he ain't give a fuck. I got the phone call from Sammy and Tommy Gunz. When I hung up the phone, I looked at your father and shot him dead in the fucking head. Don't give me this bullshit about poking the bear because your father poked the bear and it cost him his fucking life."

Animal dropped the cigar and punched K-9 in the face. Killer pulled his guns out and shot his bodyguards before they could make a move. Animal was beating the shit out of K-9. He took his gun out and started smacking him in the face with it nonstop. Animal's bodyguards pulled they guns out and was watching the doors. Animal looked down at K-9.

"Now, it's your fucking turn to die for poking the bear, pussy."

Animal shot K-9 3 times in the upper body. He then looked at Killer out of breath, gun still in is hand. "Grab the money and let's get the fuck up out of here."

Soulja hit Symone arm and pointed towards the auto shop.

"Yo, check it out. It looks like them motherfuckers got to fighting in there."

Animal and his guards rushed to the SUV and pulled off.

"Something went down in there, Soulja. Let's go check it out."

"Hell no, you tripping."

"Okay, you wait here. I'm about to go see."

Symone opened the car door and ran across the street to the auto part shop. She opened the door and went inside. That's when she saw all the blood.

"Oh shit, what the fuck," she said to herself at all the dead bodies, She then saw K-9 who was still breathing trying to reach out to her. That's when Soulja ran into the shop and saw Symone trying to help him up.

"What the fuck?"

"Get the car. We have to get him to the hospital now."

"Fuck," Soulja said as he ran to get the car.

***

"Animal, you realize you just started World War 3. You killed K-9 and his guards. It's going to be a domino effect because of this," Killer said.

"Fuck K-9 and anybody that stands with him. K-9 is dead and a dead man can't tell shit. There's no cameras in that shop. That nigga killed my father 18 years ago in that fucking shop and I just killed his pussy ass in that same fucking shop today." Animal lowered his head and looked down as he was lighting his cigar on his way back to New York.

"A dead man can't talk but you don't think he told someone about the meeting we had with him today?"

"Like I said, Killer. Fuck anybody that stands with him. I'm not hard to find."

Chapter 30

"Cash, shit was crazy. Whoever Animal went to go see, he wasn't playing real right with. He wasn't in that motherfucker 20 minutes before him and his goons came running out with guns in they hand. The same duffle they went in with they got into the SUV with and took off."

"So, y'all don't know who he went to go see?"

Soulja looked at Symone.

Cash looked at Symone. "Symone, you know his name?"

"Yeah I do. His name is K-9. I ran in the shop when Animal and his goons came running out and he was laying on the ground with bullets in his chest, still breathing."

pulled his blunt

"So, a man with holes in him just told you his name?"

"No, I told Soulja to get the car and I got him to the hospital. One of the nurses said oh my God that's K-9 when we was pulling him out the car."

"Do you think it was smart running into that shop?"

"I just wanted to see who he was going to meet and that's when I saw the dead guards and K-9 reaching out to me for help."

You might have made a power move, but only time will tell. Let's see the hand that's dealt now play out."

"So, where you need me at now Cash?"

"On the block with Smash and Solo. Show them the ropes, Soulja. Symone, you are at the trap. Test is there now."

"Cool, I'm going over there now," Symone said.

"Me too. Let me see what Smash and Solo are about."
Cash nodded as they both walked off.

***

Rude Boy walked into the auto part shop, and looked at all three dead bodies lying in pools of blood.

"What's K-9 condition?"

"From what I was told, he got shot 3 times in his shoulder, right side of his chest twice, but he's breathing."

Rude Boy looked at Snow. "Is he talking?"

"I haven't been able to see him. All I know is that Kayla called and told me that he was brought in by a female shot up."

"So, don't you think somebody need to go see the boss to find out what the fuck happened last night?"

"I'll go see him today, and if I can't talk to him, I'll have Kayla see what she can get out of him."

"Yeah, do that, and I'll have this place cleaned up."

Snow dapped up Rude Boy before walking off.

Rude Boy yelled out to him as he was leaving. "Snow."

Snow stopped and looked at him. "Yeah."

"See if she knows anything about the girl who dropped him off."

"It already crossed my mind."

Rude Boy nodded as Snow walked off.

***

"I see you do keep your word. I ain't expect to hear from you for a while or not so soon."

"Yeah, I try to keep my word in everything I do."

"How much you have in the bag, Savage? Let's talk business."

"$500,000 on the head, Mac-Ru."

Mac-Ru sucked his teeth.

"29,000 a bird. That's only going to get you 20. See, I had the understanding that you were getting 40 when you called me and said you were ready for a re-up. That means I have 20 more kilos than you can afford, Savage."

"I'll get you your money. It's only been two weeks and I came up with $580,000 for you."

"I know you good. You going to take these 20 extra birds I got and I'm going to see you in two weeks with the rest of my money. That's how we going to play this out."

"I can do that."

"Savage, have my money in two weeks. When I call, you pick up."

"I just said I'll have your money."

"I know. I'm just making it clear." Mac-Ru walked to the trunk of his car and pulled out two duffle bags and threw them on the ground in front of Savage. Savage threw the book bag on the ground next to Mac-Ru. He then picked up the two duffle bags and placed them in his car. He looked at Mac-Ru and nodded before getting inside his car driving off.

Chapter 31

K-9 opened his eyes as he was taking slow deep breaths. He looked and seen Snow standing there next to Kayla.

Snow walked up to the bed. "K-9, who did this to you?"

K-9 looked at Kayla then Snow. "Animal shot me, I want him and everything around him dead. The girl, find her. She saved my life," K-9 said in a very low tone.

"How do I find the girl?"

K-9 looked at Kayla. "She knows."

Snow looked at Kayla. "Do you know who the girl is?"

"No, I only know how she looks and I have the plate number to the car she was in."

"Good. I'm need that plate number and I'm need you to tell me how she looks."

"I can do better than that. I have a picture of her and the car she was in."

"Good, send them to me now."

"Snow, I want Animal killed."

"Done."

K-9 closed his eyes.

Snow looked at Kayla before walking out of the hospital room. He pulled his phone out and called Rude Boy.

***

Tasha looked at her phone, as it was going off. She seen the number before but she never locked it in. She couldn't remember who number it was. She looked at the number again before answering the number.

"Hello."

A soft but deep voice on the other end of the phone said, "Tasha, I see yo ain't save my number. Its K-9."

When Tasha heard his name, she got up and walked to the window and looked out of it."

"Your voice, it sounds different. Why is that?"

"So, you don't know what happened. Is what you are telling me?"

"No, what happened? I'm lost."

"Animal tried to kill me, but he failed but he did shoot me 3 times in the upper part of my body."

Tasha couldn't believe what she was hearing.

"K-9, I swear I did not know that or did I have anything to do with that."

"I know you had nothing to do with it but here's the bullet that match the gun that's put to your head right now. I'm giving you a choice right now. One, you could walk away from Animal, or two you could die with Animal."

"I told you I don't work for Animal. There's nothing to walk away from."

"Good because I have my people in New York as we speak and you don't need to catch a bullet that is meant for Animal. He don't know that I'm still alive."

"So, you called me to let me know to stay away from Animal."

"You won't mind helping me kill him?"

Tasha took a deep breath. "Respectfully, I don't want to get in between what you and Animal have going on. All I was was a driver to him. Nothing more."

K-9 was silent for a minute as he put his thoughts together. "Tasha I don't think you understand how this goes, so let me tell you. You can help me kill Animal or I can kill Animal then I can have someone help me kill you. So, what's it going to be?"

"How I know once I help you kill him that you won't kill me."

"I stand on my word. You do this, and you get a pass."

"Okay, I'll help you."

"Good." That's when there was a knock at Tasha's door. She looked at her door not knowing what to do because nobody knew she stayed there, not even Savage.

"Tasha."

"Yeah?"

"Go answer your door. My men are at your door."

Tasha opened up her door and saw Rude Boy and Snow standing there. They looked at her as they walked into her house."

"Tasha, like I told you before, my connections run deep. Animal trusts you, so you will be his weak link. My men will let you know what needs to be done, I'll talk to you soon."

K-9 hung up the phone. Tasha looked at Rude Boy and Snow, knowing she was into deep now.

***

"How we looking, Ant? What's the count on all of this?"

"300,000. We are still 280,000 short and we only have four days to get the rest of his money up."

"We running 7 blocks. We need to make more money. We are sitting on over 60 kilos of cocaine."

"Yeah but you have to remember, Cash has all of Gangster's old blocks and his still. Then you have the block beaters. They are running the other eight block. We have to knock someone out if we really want to eat."

"Yeah I know. How many shooters we have?"

"We have 6 shooters. Deadly motherfuckers that's with all the bullshit."

"Good. Tell them niggas to be on standby because shit got to go boom."

"Copy that shit. Let's pop the fucking bottle."

Savage ain't say a word he just stood there thinking.

***

Symone walked outside to her car and got inside. As she went to pull off, two black Hummers cut her off. She grabbed her gun. That's when she saw the AR-15 pointed right at her out the window of the Hummer. She placed her gun down on the seat and opened the door as one of the dudes with the AR-15 walked her to the back door of the Hummer. He opened it for her to get inside. When she looked inside, she saw K-9 sitting there eating a frozen snow cone.

"Symone, it's good to see you again."

Symone was lost for words as she looked at K-9.

"You was the guy I helped get to the hospital who was shot about 3 weeks ago."

"Bingo, you are right. Do you know who I am?"

"No, I just thought you was someone that fucked up Animal money or some shit like that."

K-9 laughed. "No baby girl, you know what I do?"

"No."

"I run shit. I'ma be in New York for a few days. You have a nice city. Let's go for a ride." That's when the back door opened to the Hummer and one of K-9 guards had Symone gun. K-9 nodded to him to give her her gun back, and car keys. She looked at K-9.

"Let me say thank you for saving my life."

"You're welcome, but how you know where to find me?"

"Like I told you I run shit. Now, let's go for a ride."

Chapter 32

The two black cars roared down the block and stopped in front of the trap spot. Ant and Savage stepped out shooting assault rifles while the other four guys came out the car shooting Glock-9s. Bodies was falling in front of the building. All you heard was the sound of guns going off. Savage was running in the building shooting whoever he seen with Ant behind him. He kicked open the trap door and yelled out, "You move you are going to fucking die. Test my gangster."

Two of the Go-Gettas had two bookbags getting all the money and drugs off the table. Savage looked at Premo who ran them blocks, pointed the gun at him and said, "News flash, this is a brand new update. Those are my fucking blocks now."

"Says who, nigga? You got me down bad right now."

"Says this AR-15, pussy." Savage pulled the trigger, letting the bullets rip through Premo's body. Blood splattered all over the back wall as bullets went through him. Savage looked at his dead body then took off running to the car and peeled off before the police hit the block.

***

Cash, Big Apple, Rip, and Soulja was all at the warehouse when K-9's two Hummers pulled up. Symone stepped out and walked up to Cash. K-9 stepped out with his man and looked around before walking towards Cash.

"You have a nice thing going on here I see."

"I do what I do. You must be K-9?"

"I am and you must be Cash. You have a loyal soulja there. They don't build them like her no more."

"She is very loyal. That's why she is the first lady respectfully. How can I help you?"

"That young lady and man over there saved my life. I owe them a debt that money can't buy. I offered her a position. She turned it down and called you. That's why we are face to face right now. Respectfully, I have some unfinished business with somebody in New York. When I'm done, I'm need a new distro for New York. Somebody that can move whatever I give them. Drugs, guns, whatever I send their way. Can that be you?"

"You are here to kill Animal. Ain't that some shit. I guess we are a lot alike because I want his fucking head too."

"I guess we are. Is that a yes, Cash? I know who you are. Let's just say my ties with people run deep."

"Yeah, that's a fucking yes."

"So come, let's go somewhere and talk and share a cigar."

"Right this way." Nobody said a word as they walked off.

***

"Animal, Tasha is at the door."

Animal puffed on his cigar before talking, "Let her in."

Killer opened the door and looked at Tasha as she walked into the apartment. She walked right by Killer up to Animal.

"You wanted to see me?"

"That's why I called you because I wanted to see you. I need you to make a run for me. It's a drop off and pick up over the bridge."

"Text me the location and I'll take care of it."

Animal pulled out his phone and texted Tasha the location.

"You going to see Jimmy. He will be waiting on you."

"Animal, this is my last run. I'm done after this."

"You're done when I tell you you are fucking done. Go make the drop and I'll see you at the pickup location, Tasha."

"Okay, Animal. I got you. I'll call you when I'm at the pickup location."

"Good. Now you see how we play ball."

"I already know. You are the coach, I'm just a player." Tasha walked out the apartment to her car, knowing Animal time was coming. She looked at the black Toyota that was across the street before driving off.

***

"Look who it is. The head nigga in charge with a bag over his shoulder. Damn, I like the way you do business motherfucker."

Savage smiled as he walked into the pool hall up to Mac-Ru.

"Like I told you before, I stand on business." Savage passed the book bag to Mac-Ru.

Mac-Ru passed the book bag to one of his little homies. "Yo, count that up and let me know how much it is, and make it fast too."

"This is what you do, play pool when you ain't on the block?"

"No, I don't play pool. I just like it up in here."

Mac-Ru little homie walked back to him. "$580,000, Mac-Ru. On the head."

Mac-Ru nodded

"He told me the count is good. I see you do stand on business. When you gon' swing back though?"

"I got some loose ends I need to tie up. Once I get that out the way, I'll make the call and let you know when is the next re-up."

"Do that, Savage. I'll be waiting to hear from you."

"I got you, homie." Savage dapped Mac-Ru up before walking off.

***

Tasha looked at the van. She stepped out of her car and got into the van. She looked around before she pulled off. It took her 2 hours to get to Harlem. She pulled up to the car dealership around back. Two white guys opened the shop doors for her to pull in. Two guys knocked on the van door.

"Hey, step out. You can have a seat over there."

Tasha got out of the van and took a seat as they was unloading the van, taking guns and drugs out, placing them on the table.

One of the guys walked up to her. "Let Animal know everything is good. Just like he said it would be. My guys are loading up the van now. You will be ready to pull out in about 20 minutes."

"Okay, and I'll let Animal know what you said."

"Thanks."

"No problem."

Tasha texted Animal and said,

I'll be driving back in 20 minutes. Everything is good on this end.

Animal replied back and said,

I'll see you at the pickup location. I'll be there when you get there.

Tasha texted him a thumbs up before getting back in the van.

***

Killer, Tasha is on the way back now. Everything went good with Jimmy. Come on, let's get the fuck up out of here. Grab them two bags because we are not coming back here."

Animal and Killer, along with 3 of his guards, all walked out of the apartment to the black Range Rover. Animal and 3 of his guards got into the Range Rover as one of his guards watched as they pulled off. Rude Boy pulled his phone out and called K-9.

K-9 picked up after a few rings. "What you have for me, Rude Boy?"

"I have eyes on Animal. He's on the move now."

"Then, let the show begin."

"You want to see the show?"

"Yeah, send me your location."

"Sharing my location now."

"I see. I'm 30 minutes away from you."

"Let me know when you are close so I can make this loud and messy."

"Just keep following him. I'll let you know when to go boom."

"Copy that."

Rude Boy hung up the phone.

"Snow, make the call to make sure everyone is on point."

Snow nodded his head and pulled his phone out.

***

Animal puffed his cigar as he looked out the window of his Range Rover. When his phone went off, he looked to see it was Jimmy calling him.

"Yeah Jimmy, I heard everything went good down there with you today." Animal lit his cigar as Jimmy started talking.

"Yeah, everything went smooth. Hey, you heard what happened to K-9 a few weeks back?"

"Yeah, it's fucked up. Did they ever find out who killed him?"

"Don't nobody know who shot him. I asked him today when I spoke to him." Animal took the cigar out of his mouth. "What you mean today when you spoke to him?"

"Yeah, I got a call about an hour ago from him. He was letting me know there are going to be a lot of new prices real soon. I asked what the fuck happened to him, and he said, just someone who poked the bear and let him live. Whatever the fuck that mean."

"You know how K-9 is. He is a tough son of a bitch but look I have some calls I need to make.

I'll call you after I do a count on what you sent me."

"Cool, let me know."

"Sure, I will."

Animal hung up the phone and looked at Killer. "I just got word that K-9 is still breathing."

"How the fuck is that? I saw you shoot him in the chest 3 times."

"I don't fucking know." Animal lowered his head and lit his blunt again.

Rude Boy got a text that said let the show begin. He smiled and cocked back his AK-47. Snow smiled holding his M16. K-9 watched as the dark blue van cut Animal's Range Rover off. The Range Rover came to a complete stop. The side of the blue van door opened up. Animal looked at the high power assault rifles that pointed at the Range Rover. He dropped his cigar as bullets came flying through the window.

Rude Boy and Snow stepped out of the car shooting the Range Rover up from the side. The windows of the Range Rover was painted with blood. K-9 stepped out of his Hummer smoking a cigar. You had people watching everything as it unfolded. Rude Boy put up his hand and made a fist. Everyone stopped shooting. The back side door opened to the Range Rover and Animal fell out, bleeding bad coughing up blood. He tried to stand up leaning on the Range

Rover. He looked at K-9 standing there smoking his cigar. Rude Boy looked at K-9. K-9 nodded. Rude Boy and everyone else opened fire on Animal. His body had over 1000 bullets running through it as blood was spraying the back of the Range Rover. Animal's body fell to the ground. Rude Boy ran up to the Range Rover and shot everyone in the head making sure they were dead. K-9 got back into his Hummer as the driver pulled off. Rude Boy and the blue van peeled out of there. Animal's body was unrecognizable from all the bullet holes and his Range Rover looked like it was painted with blood. You had over 50 people who saw the whole thing and couldn't believe what they were seeing. K-9 texted Tasha and asked her what her location was. Tasha replied back with her location.

***

Detective Cross walked around John Howard's house, taking pictures of footprints in the dirt. He went inside the house again to take a better look around trying to see how the house was broken into. He was checking to see was there any place they missed that needed to be dusted for fingerprints. After 2 hours of looking around, he walked back out the back door. He noticed a birdhouse in a tree, but there wasn't no way for the bird to get into the birdhouse. He walked up to the birdhouse and pulled it down. That's when he saw the camera inside of it.

"John Howard, you smart son of a bitch."

Detective Cross made it back to his car and pulled off headed to the police station, hoping he just found the key to breaking this case wide open.

***

K-9 stepped out of the Hummer smoking his cigar as he walked up to Tasha.

"I see you made another run for Animal."

"I did what I had to do so your men could follow him. I had to play my part."

"Play your part. I respect that. We all have a part we play to the fullest. If I'm standing here talking to you, that means I played my part."

"What you mean by that?"

"Animal is dead and everyone who stood with him are no longer breathing." Tasha looked around before talking "So, I did my part. That means we good now, right?"

"You know I did a background check on you. You are not loyal to no one but yourself."

Tasha ain't know what to say. She just looked at K-9. "How can you say that? What facts do you have?"

K-9 puffed his cigar before talking, "You know I had a long talk with Cash, and your name came up. See I know how you set up Ray-J for Gangster to kill, and how you started fucking with Animal behind Gangster back. Gangster gets killed then you start dealing with Animal. Animal tries to kill me and one phone call from me, and you helped me set up Animal to be killed. You can't be trusted."

"I do what I need to do to make it in these streets. K-9, we all have a dark path we walk. Don't judge me when you have shit under your bed still."

"I'm not judging you. I just can't let you walk out of here alive."

Tasha spit in K-9 face and took off running. K-9 shot her in the back of the head, killing her.

Rude Boy walked up to him. "Why kill her? We could have used her."

"Rude Boy, you know why a snake sheds its skin? Let me tell you, so they can be a bigger snake. Everyone she dealt with, she set up. She helped kill Ray-J, Gangster, & Animal. My name wasn't going to be on her list. Get someone to drive the van and come on, we have one more stop to make." K-9 looked at her dead body one more time before walking off.

Chapter 33

Cash was watching the news along with Big Apple and Symone.

"Damn, that fool got hit up the worst way. It have to be at least 4000 rounds in that Range Rover."

"Yeah Cash, there wasn't no surviving that. That was an over kill. Animal played with the wrong motherfucker. The top dog poured all the way out."

"Yeah Apple, I just wanted that pussy nigga blood on my hands. Thats all." Cash looked at the monitor and saw the black Hummer pulling up. He hit the button to open the garage door as K-9's driver pulled inside. K-9 stepped out, smoking a cigar.

"I see Animal's is no longer with us."

"Yeah, in this business on the level I'm on, anybody can be killed. Cash, New York City is yours now. Animal couldn't run the kingdom remember what I said."

"And what's that?"

"Animal thought he was a big dog but there's only one dog that runs the yard and that's me. K-9 don't make mistakes. Your first drop is in two weeks. Be ready. 90 days, payment is due."

"I got this. You drop this and I will take care of the rest."

"I'll be in touch." K-9 got back in his Hummer and pulled off.

Big Apple looked at Cash. "What now?"

"We run shit." Cash lowered his head and lit his blunt.

***

"Now, let's see what the fuck we got here on this SD card," Detective Cross said to himself as he placed it into his laptop. He watched as the man picked the back door open and went inside the house. He was in there for more than 2 hours, waiting on John Howard to come home. You saw the car lights from the front yard when his car pulled up. You saw the lights come on in the house. 30 minutes later, the back door opened up and the killer walks out the door. Detective Cross stopped the video and looked at his face as clear as day. He couldn't believe who he was looking at.

"You got to be fucking kidding me, but I got you now you son of a bitch and on the blood of Jesus you will never see the inside of a courtroom."

Captain Moore opened up Detecitve Cross' office door.

"Hey, any luck going back to John Howard house? Anything you can get a lead off of?"

"No, Captain. Everything was a dead fucking end. I'm back at step one again."

"Okay. Let's call it a night and you can pick up on everything tomorrow morning."

"Sure thing, Captain. I'm ready to call it a night anyway. I'm super beat."

"I'll see you tomorrow, then."

"Tomorrow, Captain."

Captain Moore closed the door. Detective Cross looked at his face one more time with hate in his eye. He then pulled the SD card out and cut the laptop off, knowing that this motherfucker was going to die in the worst fucking pain known to man. He grabbed his gun and walked out of his office.

The End

Cash lives a nefarious life, full of danger and crime, honoring the code of the street. Gangster in his trusted circle didn't honor the code of the street. Someone in Gangster's circle is playing a dirty two-faced game that draws the attention of a powerful figure. Cash and his crew ignite an all-out attack on Gangster. Gangster is forced to use every ounce of his street smarts to go toe to toe with Cash. There can only be one King in Brooklyn and Animal is determined to show Gangster and Cash that he is the one who wears the crown. He demands Cash blood but even Animal steps over the wrong line when confronting a deadly extremely powerful figures, K-9. As the heat intensifies in Brooklyn, New York, the only question stands what opps die and what opps cry.

Opps Cry 2
Standing on Business

Lock Down Publications and Ca$h Presents
Assisted Publishing Packages

Due to an increase in the price of services we have increased our prices. The prices below reflect the price increase as of 11/1/24.

BASIC PACKAGE	UPGRADED PACKAGE
$699	**$1000**
Editing	Typing
Cover Design	Editing
Formatting	Cover Design
	Formatting
	Upload eBooks to Amazon
	Upload Paperback to Amazon
ADVANCE PACKAGE	**LDP SUPREME PACKAGE**
$1,400	**$1,700**
Typing	Typing
Editing (line editing/content)	Editing (line editing/content)
Cover Design	Cover Design
Formatting	Formatting
Copyright Registration	Copyright Registration
Proofreading	Proofreading
Upload eBooks to Amazon	Set up Amazon Account
Upload Paperback to Amazon	Upload eBooks to Amazon
	Upload Paperback to Amazon
	Advertise on LDP's Amazon and Facebook Page

***Other services available upon request.
Additional charges may apply

Lock Down Publications
P.O. Box 944
Stockbridge, GA 30281-9998
Phone: 470 303-9761
Email: lockdownpublications@gmail.com

142

Submission Guideline

Submit the first three chapters of your completed manuscript to ldpsubmissions@gmail.com. In the subject line add **Your Book's Title**. The manuscript must be in a Word Doc file and sent as an attachment. Document should be in Times New Roman, double spaced, and in size 12 font. Also, provide your synopsis and full contact information. If sending multiple submissions, they must each be in a separate email.

Have a story but no way to send it electronically? You can still submit to LDP/Ca$h Presents. Send in the first three chapters, written or typed, of your completed manuscript to:

LDP: Submissions Dept
P.O. Box 944
Stockbridge, GA 30281-9998

DO NOT send original manuscript. Must be a duplicate.
Provide your synopsis and a cover letter containing your full contact information.

Thanks for considering LDP and Ca$h Presents.

NEW RELEASES

BLOODLINE OF A SAVAGE 1,2&3
THESE VICIOUS STREETS 1,2&3
RELENTLESS GOON
RELENTLESS GOON 2
BY PRINCE A. TAUHID

THE BUTTERFLY MAFIA 1-3
BY FUMIYA PAYNE

A THUG'S STREET PRINCESS 1,2&3
BY MEESHA

CITY OF SMOKE 1& 2
BY MOLOTTI

STEPPERS 1,2&3
THE REAL BADDIES OF CHI-RAQ
BY KING RIO

THE LANE 1&2
BY KEN-KEN SPENCE

THUG OF SPADES 1,2&3
LOVE IN THE TRENCHES 2
CORNER BOY CHRONICLES
BY COREY ROBINSON

TIL DEATH 3
BY ARYANNA

THE BIRTH OF A GANGSTER 4
BY DELMONT PLAYER

PRODUCT OF THE STREETS 1&2
BY DEMOND "MONEY" ANDERSON

NO TIME FOR ERROR
BY KEESE

MONEY HUNGRY DEMONS 1,2&3
BY TRANAY ADAMS

HUNGRY FOR MONEY 1&2
BY SLIMBOS

A THUGGISH PASSION
KILLAZ ON STANDBY 1&2
LAND OF DA HOOLIGANZ 1,2&3
FRESH OFF DA PORCH
BY IRA B.

COUNTDOWN OF A KILLA 1&2
GUNS DOWN, BOTTOMS UP 1&2
SEX, MURDA AND GOD
BY LO-LIFE

THE LEVEL UP 1&2
BY LUXURY KING

FO'EVA ROLLIN' 1&2
BY ASSA RAYMOND BAKER

HUB CITY MENACE 1&2
BY J. WHITE

KILLA CREW
DYING FOR LIKES
BY ARYANNA

IF YOU CROSS ME ONCE 6
ANGEL 5
By Anthony Fields

IMMA DIE BOUT MINE 5
By Aryanna

A THUGS STREET PRINCESS 3
EMBRACING THE LOVE OF A BOSS
By Meesha

PRODUCT OF THE STREETS 3
By Demond Money Anderson

STANDING ON HER BUSINESS
BY DG SANTANA

GET IT IN SLUGS 1&2
B. STALLS

CORNER BOYS 2
By Corey Robinson

THE MURDER QUEENS 6&7
By Michael Gallon

CITY OF SMOKE 3
By Molotti

CONFESSIONS OF A DOPEBOY
By Nicholas Lock

TENDER
BY KHUFU

THA TAKEOVER
By Keith Chandler

BETRAYAL OF A G 2
By Ray Vinci

CRIME BOSS 4
By Playa Ray

Coming Soon from Lock Down Publications/Ca$h Presents

RAN OFF ON THE PLUG 2 by **PAPER BOI RARI**
STREET REDEMPTION by **TONY DANIELS**
SAVAGE FAMILY EMPIRE by **PRINCE TAUHID**
BAD BITCHES WIT' GUNZ by **DIESEL**
THE SINGLE LADIES by **DIESEL**
COKE BY THE TRUCKLOAD by **DIESEL**
PROBLEM SOLVED by **DIESEL**
TIPPIN' THE SCALES by **DIESEL**
OPPS CRY TOO by **SAYNOMORE**
A GANGSTA'S KARMA by **FLAME**

AVAILABLE NOW

RESTRAINING ORDER 1 & 2
By **CA$H & Coffee**

LOVE KNOWS NO BOUNDARIES 1-3
By **Coffee**

RAISED AS A GOON I, II, III & IV
BRED BY THE SLUMS I, II, III
BLAST FOR ME I & II
ROTTEN TO THE CORE I II III
A BRONX TALE I, II, III
DUFFLE BAG CARTEL I II III IV V VI
HEARTLESS GOON I II III IV V
A SAVAGE DOPEBOY I II
DRUG LORDS I II III
CUTTHROAT MAFIA I II
KING OF THE TRENCHES
By **Ghost**

LAY IT DOWN I & II
LAST OF A DYING BREED I II
BLOOD STAINS OF A SHOTTA I & II III
By **Jamaica**

LOYAL TO THE GAME I II III
LIFE OF SIN I, II III
By **TJ & Jelissa**

IF LOVING HIM IS WRONG…I & II
LOVE ME EVEN WHEN IT HURTS I II III
By **Jelissa**

OPPS CRY TOO 2 | SAYNOMORE

PUSH IT TO THE LIMIT
By **Bre' Hayes**

BLOODY COMMAS I & II
SKI MASK CARTEL I, II & III
KING OF NEW YORK I II, III IV V
RISE TO POWER I II III
COKE KINGS I II III IV V
BORN HEARTLESS I II III IV
KING OF THE TRAP I II
By **T.J. Edwards**

WHEN THE STREETS CLAP BACK I & II III
THE HEART OF A SAVAGE I II III IV
MONEY MAFIA I II
LOYAL TO THE SOIL I II III
By **Jibril Williams**

A DISTINGUISHED THUG STOLE MY HEART I - III
LOVE SHOULDN'T HURT I II III IV
RENEGADE BOYS 1-4
PAID IN KARMA 1-3
SAVAGE STORMS 1-3
AN UNFORESEEN LOVE 1-3
BABY, I'M WINTERTIME COLD 1-3
A THUG'S STREET PRINCESS 1&2
By **Meesha**

CUM FOR ME 1-8
An LDP Erotica Collaboration

BLOOD OF A BOSS 1-5
SHADOWS OF THE GAME
TRAP BASTARD
By **Askari**

A GANGSTER'S CODE 1-3
A GANGSTER'S SYN 1-3
THE SAVAGE LIFE 1-3
CHAINED TO THE STREETS 1-3
BLOOD ON THE MONEY 1-3
A GANGSTA'S PAIN 1-3
BEAUTIFUL LIES AND UGLY TRUTHS
CHURCH IN THESE STREETS
By **J-Blunt**

THE STREETS BLEED MURDER 1-3
THE HEART OF A GANGSTA 1-3
By **Jerry Jackson**

WHEN A GOOD GIRL GOES BAD
By **Adrienne**

THE COST OF LOYALTY 1-3
By **Kweli**

BRIDE OF A HUSTLA 1-3
THE FETTI GIRLS 1-3
CORRUPTED BY A GANGSTA 1-4
BLINDED BY HIS LOVE
THE PRICE YOU PAY FOR LOVE 1-3
DOPE GIRL MAGIC 1-3
By **Destiny Skai**

A KINGPIN'S AMBITION
A KINGPIN'S AMBITION II
I MURDER FOR THE DOUGH
By **Ambitious**

A DOPEBOY'S PRAYER
By **Eddie "Wolf" Lee**

TRUE SAVAGE 1-7
DOPE BOY MAGIC 1-3
MIDNIGHT CARTEL 1-3
CITY OF KINGZ 1&2
NIGHTMARE ON SILENT AVE
THE PLUG OF LIL MEXICO 1&2
CLASSIC CITY
By **Chris Green**

LOVE & CHASIN' PAPER
By **Qay Crockett**

THE KING CARTEL 1-3
By **Frank Gresham**

THESE NIGGAS AIN'T LOYAL 1-3
By **Nikki Tee**

GANGSTA SHYT 1-3
By **CATO**

THE ULTIMATE BETRAYAL
By **Phoenix**

BOSS'N UP 1-3
By **Royal Nicole**

I LOVE YOU TO DEATH
By **Destiny J**

BROOKLYN HUSTLAZ
By **Boogsy Morina**

GANGSTA CITY
By **Teddy Duke**

TO DIE IN VAIN
SINS OF A HUSTLA
By **ASAD**

I RIDE FOR MY HITTA
I STILL RIDE FOR MY HITTA
By **Misty Holt**

A GANGSTER'S REVENGE 1-4
THE BOSS MAN'S DAUGHTERS 1-5
A SAVAGE LOVE 1&2
BAE BELONGS TO ME 1&2
A HUSTLER'S DECEIT 1-3
WHAT BAD BITCHES DO 1-3
SOUL OF A MONSTER 1-3
KILL ZONE
A DOPE BOY'S QUEEN 1-3
TIL DEATH 1-3
IMMA DIE BOUT MINE 1-5
By **Aryanna**

BROOKLYN ON LOCK 1 & 2
By **Sonovia**

A DRUG KING AND HIS DIAMOND 1-3
A DOPEMAN'S RICHES
HER MAN, MINE'S TOO 1&2
CASH MONEY HO'S
THE WIFEY I USED TO BE 1&2
PRETTY GIRLS DO NASTY THINGS
By **Nicole Goosby**

THE STREETS ARE CALLING
By **Duquie Wilson**

LIPSTICK KILLAH 1-3
CRIME OF PASSION 1-3
FRIEND OR FOE 1-3
By **Mimi**

TRAPHOUSE KING 1-3
KINGPIN KILLAZ 1-3
STREET KINGS 1&2
PAID IN BLOOD 1&2
CARTEL KILLAZ 1-3
DOPE GODS 1&2
By **Hood Rich**

STEADY MOBBN' 1-3
THE STREETS STAINED MY SOUL 1-3
By **Marcellus Allen**

WHO SHOT YA 1-3
SON OF A DOPE FIEND 1-4
HEAVEN GOT A GHETTO 1&2
SKI MASK MONEY 1&2
By **Renta**

GORILLAZ IN THE BAY 1-4
TEARS OF A GANGSTA 1/&2
3X KRAZY 1&2
STRAIGHT BEAST MODE 1&2
By **DE'KARI**

TRIGGADALE 1-3
MURDA WAS THE CASE 1-3
By **Elijah R. Freeman**

MARRIED TO A BOSS 1-3
By **Destiny Skai & Chris Green**

SLAUGHTER GANG 1-3
RUTHLESS HEART 1-3
By **Willie Slaughter**

GOD BLESS THE TRAPPERS 1-3
THESE SCANDALOUS STREETS 1-3
FEAR MY GANGSTA 1-5
THESE STREETS DON'T LOVE NOBODY 1-2
BURY ME A G 1-5
A GANGSTA'S EMPIRE 1-4
THE DOPEMAN'S BODYGAURD 1&2
THE REALEST KILLAZ 1-3
THE LAST OF THE OGS 1-3
By **Tranay Adams**

KINGZ OF THE GAME 1-7
CRIME BOSS 1-4
By **Playa Ray**

FUK SHYT
By **Blakk Diamond**

DON'T F#CK WITH MY HEART 1&2
By **Linnea**

ADDICTED TO THE DRAMA 1-3
IN THE ARM OF HIS BOSS
By **Jamila**

LOYALTY AIN'T PROMISED 1&2
By **Keith Williams**

FOREVER GANGSTA 1&2
GLOCKS ON SATIN SHEETS 1&2
By **Adrian Dulan**

YAYO 1-4
A SHOOTER'S AMBITION 1&2
BRED IN THE GAME
By **S. Allen**

TRAP GOD 1-3
RICH $AVAGE 1-3
MONEY IN THE GRAVE 1-3
CARTEL MONEY
By **Martell Troublesome Bolden**

TOE TAGZ 1-4
LEVELS TO THIS SHYT 1&2
IT'S JUST ME AND YOU
By **Ah'Million**

KINGPIN DREAMS 1-3
RAN OFF ON DA PLUG
By **Paper Boi Rari**

THE STREETS MADE ME 1-3
By **Larry D. Wright**

CONFESSIONS OF A GANGSTA 1-4
CONFESSIONS OF A JACKBOY 1-3
CONFESSIONS OF A HITMAN
By **Nicholas Lock**

I'M NOTHING WITHOUT HIS LOVE
SINS OF A THUG
TO THE THUG I LOVED BEFORE
A GANGSTA SAVED XMAS
IN A HUSTLER I TRUST
By **Monet Dragun**

QUIET MONEY 1-3
THUG LIFE 1-3
EXTENDED CLIP 1&2
A GANGSTA'S PARADISE
By **Trai'Quan**

CAUGHT UP IN THE LIFE 1-3
THE STREETS NEVER LET GO 1-3
By **Robert Baptiste**

NEW TO THE GAME 1-3
MONEY, MURDER & MEMORIES 1-3
By **Malik D. Rice**

THE LIFE OF A HOOD STAR
By **Ca$h & Rashia Wilson**

THE STREETS WILL NEVER CLOSE 1-4
By **K'ajji**

LIFE OF A SAVAGE 1-4
A GANGSTA'S QUR'AN 1-4
MURDA SEASON 1-3
GANGLAND CARTEL 1-3
CHI'RAQ GANGSTAS 1-4
KILLERS ON ELM STREET 1-3
JACK BOYZ N DA BRONX 1-3
A DOPEBOY'S DREAM 1-3
JACK BOYS VS DOPE BOYS 1-3
COKE GIRLZ
COKE BOYS
SOSA GANG 1&2
BRONX SAVAGES
BODYMORE KINGPINS
BLOOD OF A GOON
By **Romell Tukes**

CREAM 2-3
THE STREETS WILL TALK
By **Yolanda Moore**

CONCRETE KILLA 1-3
VICIOUS LOYALTY 1-3
By **Kingpen**

THE ULTIMATE SACRIFICE 1-6
KHADIFI
IF YOU CROSS ME ONCE 1-5
ANGEL 1-4
IN THE BLINK OF AN EYE
By **Anthony Fields**

NIGHTMARES OF A HUSTLA 1-3
BLOOD AND GAMES 1&2
By **King Dream**

HARD AND RUTHLESS 1&2
MOB TOWN 251
THE BILLIONAIRE BENTLEYS 1-3
REAL G'S MOVE IN SILENCE
By **Von Diesel**

MOB TIES 1-7
SOUL OF A HUSTLER, HEART OF A KILLER 1-3
GORILLAZ IN THE TRENCHES
By **SayNoMore**

BODYMORE MURDERLAND 1-3
THE BIRTH OF A GANGSTER 1-4
By **Delmont Player**

FOR THE LOVE OF A BOSS 1&2
By **C. D. Blue**

KILLA KOUNTY 1-5
By **Khufu**

MOBBED UP 1-4
THE BRICK MAN 1-5
THE COCAINE PRINCESS 1-10
STEPPERS 1-3
SUPER GREMLIN 1-4
By **King Rio**

MONEY GAME 1&2
By **Smoove Dolla**

A GANGSTA'S KARMA 1-4
By **FLAME**

KING OF THE TRENCHES 1-3
By **GHOST & TRANAY ADAMS**

QUEEN OF THE ZOO 1&2
By **Black Migo**

GRIMEY WAYS 1-3
BETRAYAL OF A G
By **Ray Vinci**

XMAS WITH AN ATL SHOOTER
By **Ca$h & Destiny Skai**

KING KILLA 1&2
By **Vincent "Vitto" Holloway**

BETRAYAL OF A THUG 1&2
By **Fre$h**

OPPS CRY TOO 2 | SAYNOMORE

THE MURDER QUEENS 1-6
By **Michael Gallon**

FOR THE LOVE OF BLOOD 1-4
By **Jamel Mitchell**

HOOD CONSIGLIERE 1&2
NO TIME FOR ERROR
By **Keese**

PROTÉGÉ OF A LEGEND 1&2
LOVE IN THE TRENCHES 1&2
By **Corey Robinson**

THE PLUG'S RUTHLESS DAUGHTER 1&2
By **Tony Daniels**

BORN IN THE GRAVE 1-3
CRIME PAYS 1&2
By **Self Made Tay**

MOAN IN MY MOUTH
By **XTASY**

TORN BETWEEN A GANGSTER AND A
GENTLEMAN
By **J-BLUNT & Miss Kim**

HERE TODAY GONE TOMORROW 1&2
By **Fly Rock**

PILLOW PRINCESS
By **S. Hawkins**

SANCTIFIED AND HORNY
by **XTASY**

WOMEN LIE MEN LIE 1-4
FIFTY SHADES OF SNOW 1-3
STACK BEFORE YOU SPLURGE
GIRLS FALL LIKE DOMINOES
NAÏVE TO THE STREETS
By **ROY MILLIGAN**

LOYALTY IS EVERYTHING 1-3
CITY OF SMOKE 1&2
By **Molotti**

THE BUTTERFLY MAFIA 1-4
SALUTE MY SAVAGERY 1&2
By **Fumiya Payne**

THE LANE 1&2
By **Ken-Ken Spence**

THE PUSSY TRAP 1-5
By **Nene Capri**

DIRTY DNA
By **Blaque**

BOOKS BY LDP'S CEO, CA$H

TRUST IN NO MAN
TRUST IN NO MAN 2
TRUST IN NO MAN 3
BONDED BY BLOOD
SHORTY GOT A THUG
THUGS CRY
THUGS CRY 2
THUGS CRY 3
TRUST NO BITCH
TRUST NO BITCH 2
TRUST NO BITCH 3
TIL MY CASKET DROPS
RESTRAINING ORDER
RESTRAINING ORDER 2
IN LOVE WITH A CONVICT
LIFE OF A HOOD STAR
XMAS WITH AN ATL SHOOTER

www.ingramcontent.com/pod-product-compliance
Lightning Source LLC
Chambersburg PA
CBHW071222260626
47162CB00004B/1398